I0588069

This is a work of fiction. Names, characters, businesses, places, events,
locales, and incidents are either the products of the author's imagination
or used in a fictitious manner. Any resemblance to actual persons, living
or dead, or actual events is purely coincidental.

fraud(pr)ess
All rights reserved.
©2021 Holly Manno
www.fraudpress.love
www.lovetest.love

TIMES TWO

HOLLY MANNO

Edited by
JENNIFER L ROOP

www.frankpress.love

MATCHMAKING DESTINY

Matchmaking Destiny with www.lovetest.love
By Ryan Glass

WITH EVERYTHING that's happened over the past few days, I find it hard to sit still, let alone compose my thoughts about a sequence of events that has forever changed my path. I am no romantic. I've often reported on the darker side of humanity and because of that, I didn't intend to marry. Destiny, God, chance, www.lovetest.love, my boss—whatever label you have for it, something inter-vened and the ripples of my journey have created wakes of change for others. My family has grown, my friendships are wider, and I've found love so enormous it scares me.

YOU KNOW HOW THEY SAY, *All's well that ends well?* You'll have to keep reading to find out how this one ends. One thing I've learned is how one small incident can alter the course of lives forever. This tale sounds like fiction, but it's not.

LOVE TEST

The geese honked loudly and the aroma of coffee filled the air. Lanie stirred in the soft grey covers and slowly opened her eyes. From the mezzanine loft, she looked through the peaked wall of glass and onto the Columbia river. Steel grey water lapped against the dock and the barren trees swayed in the cool November wind.

"Rise and shine," Ryan's voice chimed as he ascended the floating stairs.

She adjusted herself to sitting as he entered the bedroom with a tray in hand. He placed it on her lap and kissed her lips with three soft pecks.

She smiled sweetly while leering at his bare chest and taught abdominals, "Good morning, husband."

His cheeks dimpled in a glorious smile, "Good morning, wife." He plucked a grape from the tray and held it temptingly near Lanie's mouth. Her eyes bore into his, causing an instant rise in his pajama pants. "Keep looking at me that way and you're going to make me late for work."

Her green eyes held as she purred, "What's work?"

"I have to admit," Ryan's tone was steady as he pinched her nipple through her silken slip, "I like what pregnancy has done for our sex life." With that he tossed the grape and devoured her mouth with a wake-up kiss.

A moan escaped her throat as he pinched a little harder, then pulled back. His forehead rested against hers. She panted, "I've wanted you every moment from the first time I saw you."

His hands cuffed both of her wrists as he whispered, "Breakfast first, little wife. You are eating for two and you're going to need some energy."

Her simpering expression made it almost impossible for him to retreat. "After breakfast then?"

He chuckled, a now familiar sound that tickled her ears, "Try to stop me." He held a forkful of eggs and spinach to her mouth.

She took the utensil from him, "I can still feed myself."

He smirked and circled the bed to join her on the other side.

Lanie held the oversized mug that contained her decaf latte and asked, "What's on your agenda today?"

"Staff meeting, some research, the usual. By the way, did you get the email from Erve about the www.lovetest.love event? Are you all set for prom night? Have you prepared for our interviews?"

Lanie shook her head and replaced the mug on the tray as Ryan plucked a piece of bacon from the plate. "Remind me again how we got roped into being masters of ceremony for this."

Ryan cocked his head to one side and reached for Lanie's belly. Resting a hand on her stomach, he said, "It all started with this dating app and a very curious little artist. So curious in fact, that a journalist who was covering the event couldn't take his eyes off of her. After a challenging beginning, they both realized they belonged together. His boss agreed and forced the journalist to write a newspaper column, which went viral. And now they live happily ever after."

Lanie worked up a pout, "I think someone left out a few details. For example, where did they live happily ever after?"

Her comment brought forward the question they'd been grappling with for months. "Where indeed," he repeated. "I've set up a meeting with Isabell, the realtor, for Sunday if that helps."

Her eyes fell to the tray. "I'm not sure if it helps, but it is the first step. Thanks for arranging it."

"Hey," Ryan rested a finger under her chin, "don't look so down. House hunting is supposed to be fun."

"I know," she agreed. "It's just great the way it is. I love splitting time between our homes. They're both so different. It's like we're always on vacation. Once we buy a house together, things will change. I'm sure it will be great. I just can't imagine how we'll be living. I don't want to become a suburbanite just because we're having a baby."

RYAN UNDERSTOOD HER FEELINGS. Lately he'd been having the same thoughts. He was hesitant about leaving his place and the serenity it provided. After his international assignments, he'd always looked forward to the healing he found in this home, to watching the world pass slowly through the plate of glass. He wouldn't echo her concerns so instead he consoled, "Lanie, it's us. Whatever home we find, it will represent you and me. It has to or it won't be ours."

She nodded slowly, "I know. It's just hard to imagine selling my place, or this one. Separately, we've created so much in our homes, and it's where our marriage began. So many changes…" She teared up.

Ryan cooed, "Hey, what's wrong?"

He nuzzled her neck and the tears subsided. "Pregnancy, I guess. You have your little son or daughter to blame."

His kisses tickled. "I'm glad we decided to be surprised about the sex and I can't wait to meet him or her, but right now, I need to ravish their mommy." Abruptly, Ryan plucked the tray from her lap and placed it on the nightstand.

He returned to the bedside and sat facing her. The strap of her navy silk nightie teetered from her shoulder. His world-blue eyes bore into hers as his finger gently trailed the strap. Her chest rose and fell more rapidly and her nipples became taught as they pushed through the thin sheen of satin. His feather soft caresses barely touched her skin yet the heat began to rise. "On your knees," he rasped.

She moved to kneel and he swiftly tugged the slip over her head, exposing her naked body. The swell of their child was no longer hidden. Her breasts were even larger than usual, her nipples darker. She had never looked hotter to him. His manhood was like a beacon pointed toward his jewel.

She slid his pants down to expose his need. Her mouth twitched and her hands were unstoppable as she circled him, using the soft pad of her thumb to tease. His head tipped back as her mouth took over. Ryan couldn't handle it for long. His hands pushed against her shoulders and she released him. A moment later he faced her on the bed. His mouth covered hers and his fingers teased her spot. She whined, "I want you, now."

He rasped, "Lay on your side."

She didn't wait and he was right behind her, spooning

her. His hands tortured her needy bosom as she panted. Ryan couldn't wait any longer. He guided himself inside of her and with his free hand he collared her throat.

She accepted him and tried to hold her frenzied desire at bay. With the smallest move, she arched her low back to accommodate his closeness. In every breath they found a way to reach even deeper, get nearer, and feel more until they were one breath, one sigh, one body. He touched her everywhere and she gave him license to do it forever, however and whenever he chose. She was no longer herself. She was Ryan's woman, his wife, and soon-to-be mother of his child. He could have anything she had and more.

Ryan felt her submission with every stroke. He wanted to possess her, to command her, and for every cell in her body to feel him. Their fingers intertwined—which were hers and which were his? The breath between them, those sounds, that heat, mine, hers? No, ours. She tightened around him and he stiffened beyond straining. The ecstasy was too great. Her scream filled the house and they exploded at once. As the last ravages of aftershock ripped through them, his promise was laced by the love in his voice, "This is ours. It will never change."

THOUGH IT WAS before 8 a.m., the newsroom teemed with life. Ryan marched up the corridor to his office with his head ducked. Flipping on the lights, he dropped his laptop bag and pulled the composition book from the side pocket. It was the latest of the hundreds that Ryan had filled over the years. Everything he'd ever written was first scribbled on a piece of paper.

He removed his pen from the bag, the one Lanie had

inscribed as a wedding present. His fingers smoothed over the wooden cap and pressed against the golden lettering. *"I am yours, forever."* He smiled inwardly and tried to suppress the devious flashback from their morning lovemaking.

Clink, clink, clink, the sound of knuckles against glass got his attention. "Morning, sir," Erve's tone was taunting. "Glad you could join us."

Ryan strode toward the door, "Good morning, boss. I'm just in time for the staff meeting."

Erve glanced at his watch and stated blandly, "Just. Let's go kid."

They walked into the conference room. Erve settled at the head of the table, while Ryan found a seat in the middle. "Good morning, everyone. We've got a lot to do. Marketing, do you want to start us off? Give us an update on print and web sales."

"Sure," Fae piped up and she started in on the latest advertisers, deadlines, and outstanding issues. Ryan let his thoughts drift back to his earlier conversation with Lanie. He didn't show her they shared similar concerns, but with time to reflect, he had to admit, he was hesitant to leave the home he'd built and the foundation they'd started together. Since they met, things had moved at an unexpected pace. They were married in under a year, and in a matter of months, their first child would arrive. He reminded himself that everything moved fast for a reason. They fit.

Still, the idea of finding a four-bedroom house in the right school district wasn't exciting to him either. With the added stress of a large mortgage, selling their homes, and the baby's arrival, he was feeling less than ready, but he wanted her to know she'd chosen a strong husband, thus his brave words when she raised the subject.

"Ryan, Ryan?" a wad of paper hit his sternum simultaneous to Erve's grating call.

He cleared his throat, "Yes, boss."

"Will you give everyone a rundown on the www.lovetest.love contest? We're all dying to know how the prom king and his beautiful queen will be approaching the event and the column."

Ryan nodded, "Sure, sure. You all know how www.lovetest.love works. It's an algorithm-based matchmaking system that excludes photos and direct messaging. Instead, the system matches people based on the compatibility profile. Candidates with the highest potential are invited to these glitzy networking parties where they meet in person. Lanie and I are the emcees for their upcoming one-year anniversary celebration.

"As a special kicker, they're giving away a prize that comes with a test. The top two matches selected by the algorithm will continue the experiment by going on five fantasy dates. For a little extra drama, the final one is on Valentine's Day. On that day, the couples will declare to the world, via live broadcast, their intentions to 'stay or go.'

"There are 30 contestants or potential matches. Half of them identify as male and the other half as female. We're doing a speed interview before the mixer. Lanie and I will spend three minutes with each contestant. We're going to ask six questions, three apiece. In the end, we'll compare notes and make our best guess on the two most likely couples. Our answers will be tallied with the computer's algorithm and that will determine the winners.

"Any questions?"

The room was in flux as questions piled over each other.

"Can I get an invite?"

"What questions will you ask"

"Who died and made you Cupid?"

"Enough, enough, everyone quiet." Erve's voice cut through the room. "Ryan, you'll be writing five articles, one about the winners and for each of the date. The final interview with all of the winners will be a live broadcast. Be sure to alternate perspectives between the women and the men and send me the schedule this afternoon. We'll print on Sundays a week after each date." His eyes danced with excitement, "If we play this right, this could be just what we need to boost sales through the holidays and start next year with a bang. Everyone loves love."

"Sure, boss." Ryan's brows rose.

"Oh, and send me your interview questions."

Ryan nodded then remembered he and Lanie had yet to compose their questions. Sliding his phone from his pocket, he quickly sent her a text. "Our questions for the interview…we need to put them together."

Three dots indicated she was working on a reply. "Yes, sir. I'll have them for you by lunch. xxx"

"Good girl. I'll show you my appreciation tonight."

———

LANIE SLID her phone back into her purse and pulled the large glass door to the gallery open. Jay was standing at the back brewing a cup of espresso. "Good morning, boss lady."

"Mornin', Jay." She chimed.

He whistled, "Don't you look hot."

She wore a camel colored sweater dress, empire style, and a matching overcoat with brown boots. Breezing past him on the way to her desk, she said, "Thanks, Jay. I'm feeling pretty hot today."

His eyes crinkled from a knowing smile. "Pregnancy does agree with you."

"What do you want to drink? I've made a new batch of your elixir. This time I added Som Cordial. It has turmeric in it. I can put it in your herbal tea."

"Sounds good, thanks." Lanie put her purse away and went about logging onto her computer, asking him, "How are you doing today?

He added a tea bag to her steel lined coffee cup and poured steaming hot water over it. "I'm well."

Not only the brevity sent a warning, but the higher octave he used in his reply assured Lanie there was something amiss. She didn't mince words, "What is it?"

He added a health shot to her tumbler and placed the lid on top. Walking to face her, he gently set the mug down and blurted, "Serge wants to get married."

"What? Wow," she exclaimed. "That's amazing. Congratulations."

Jay's expression was unreadable.

"Wait, you don't want to get married?" she asked more than stated.

Jay's sharp intake of breath was followed by the shuffle of his feet. "I, I don't know. Honestly, I never thought I would. It didn't occur to me that I could or that I should. We both know how I used to be."

Lanie's reply was a plea, " I do, but I also see you've changed a lot in the past year. You and Serge are solid. In fact, you're slipping. You missed a hot guy at Café Umbria the other day."

"Oh, the brooding brunet with the perfectly straight nose? I noticed. I just didn't say anything. What's the point —I'm not available, so why go there?"

She pursed her lips, "How are things with you and Serge, really?"

Jay paced a few steps and turned. "They're great. Ideal actually. Our schedules work so we have plenty of time together, but we still get our solitude. We like the same things, music, food, sex. It's all…gorgeous."

"So, what's the problem?"

Jay shook his head, "The usual I guess. It's good the way it is. What if getting married changes things? And what if I can't do it?"

"Do what?"

"Be faithful."

"Is that really what worries you?"

"What if he can't either?"

"That's a lot of what if's Jay. The unanswerable kind. How do you feel about him?"

"I love him. I can't picture a day without him. Even when I'm pissed off at him, I'm still excited to wake up next to him."

Lanie stood and circled the desk. Standing in front of Jay, she smiled into his crystal blue eyes, "Then what are you waiting for? Say yes and let's plan a wedding."

He smiled with more assurance than doubt, "Give me a second to think about this. Maybe I will." As if his life depended upon it, he changed the subject. Resting a hand on her stomach he asked, "Are you getting excited about the Love Test prom?"

She shook her head. "Not really. In fact, I have to put a few questions together this morning."

"Questions?" Jay asked.

"Yes, Ryan and I are interviewing the candidates and we are going to ask the same questions of everyone. We're going to use the questions to help us guess which couples will make the best match. Our answers will be added to the algorithm and that will determine the winning couples."

Jay shook his head. "Look at what you've done. Your

dating experiment has gone viral and you've morphed into a romance expert just as you are about to become a mother."

Lanie huffed in reply, "Ha, ha. Well, since I'm such an expert, you should listen to me and marry Serge. Until then, I know you're dying to give me a hand with these questions."

Jay rubbed his hands excitedly, "You are right about that."

On a dreary Thursday morning in November, two friends put their heads together to compile the list of questions that would set and reset a course to love.

Questions for the Love Test Interviews:

What is your favorite holiday memory and why?

Describe your perfect Sunday with your significant other.

What's the most embarrassing thing you've ever done?

What's one decision you've made that you'd like to go back and change?

If you meet the love of your life and they hurt you, how would you handle it?

What is your biggest fear?

3

LET THE GAMES BEGIN

The Hotel Monaco thrived with energy from the thirty well-groomed singles who'd set out to meet their match at the exclusive www.lovetest.love first annual event. The room was decorated with fun velvet furniture and warmed by a roaring fire and flickering that candles that rested on every surface. It felt like romance.

Ryan and Lanie stood on the stage against a backdrop of deep fuchsia walls. He tapped the mic and said, "Good evening."

The room went quiet.

"I'm Ryan Glass and this is my beautiful wife Lanie. Welcome to the first annual www.lovetest.love contest."

The room erupted with claps and cheers.

Ryan held up his hand. "As you know, this is a very special evening, not only to the creators of www.lovetest.love, but for my wife and I personally. You see," he looked at Lanie and took her hand, "this event is where I first saw her, just over a year ago. Had it not been for the circumstances that sprung out of me covering this exciting matchmaking concept, I'd have missed meeting the most amazing woman."

The crowd went crazy.

Lanie kissed Ryan on the cheek and took the microphone. "We wish the same kind of life-changing connection to all of you. Our journey wasn't easy, but we're happier than we've ever imagined and it all started with a love test. Are you ready to begin?"

There was more clapping from the crowd.

Ryan cleared his throat. "Here's how it is going to work. Lanie and I will be speed interviewing each of you. You'll have three minutes to answer our questions. After our meeting with you, we'll give our best suggestion about which couples we think fit. Our feedback will be combined with the data from your profile algorithm. The couples with the highest compatibility will win five incredible dates. The fifth date will end with a live broadcast where the chosen couples will tell us if they intend to stay together or go their separate ways."

Screams, claps, and hoots filled the room.

Lanie raised her hand this time. "Keep in mind, we are not matchmakers. Ryan and I are doing this for fun and to weigh in on the human side, but the algorithm is the engine. We hope you'll have an open heart and trust this fun process that's combining technology and destiny. Until you're called, please mingle. Interviews start in five!"

They left the stage as the final round of clapping faded and the singles began to mill around. "This way, guys," pointed the event coordinator, Shelly. "You'll be in here and we'll keep the crowd moving. Lanie, you take this side and we'll start you with the ladies." She waved toward a red velvet chair and single table with a black cloth over it.

Pointing to a table at the other side of a partition, Shelly said, "Ryan, you'll sit here and we'll send them your way. After the first round of contestants, we'll give you a ten-minute break before we send the second group through.

"We'll need about fifteen minutes after we receive your answers to tally the winners. Any questions?"

"None for me," Lanie answered.

"I'm good too, " Ryan replied.

"Great, well, get settled, I'll send your first interview in in five." Shelly vanished through the door.

Ryan put his arm around Lanie and walked toward her table. Pulling the chair for her, he solicited, "Ms. Cupid."

She smiled deviously, a leer really, as her eyes ran up and down the length of his body. She came near, nuzzled his neck, and whispered, "Sexy as you look in it, I can't wait to get you out of that suit." She didn't linger and quickly took her seat.

As if in slow motion, Ryan hovered at her neck while pushing in the chair. Lanie knew she was on display. The emerald maxi dress she wore exposed her stunning décolletage. His breath teased her flesh as he inched her forward.

Like a bucket of ice, the door swung wide and Shelly re-entered. "Two minutes."

Ryan jumped from the interruption and smiled like an idiot. "Yep, we're ready."

Shelly shook her head and exited the room as Ryan scurried to the other side of the partition.

Lanie took a moment to review the questions she would be asking. Pen in hand, she smiled and laughed to herself about the idea that she could be a matchmaker. After all, she was engaged to another man when she set up a Love Test profile.

There wasn't much time to linger as a cheery blonde

took a seat across from her. "Hi, I'm Dawn and I'm ready for the test."

The time passed quickly as Lanie rushed through the questions, finding a rhythm with many of the answers. It was interesting how many people replied generically and though they responded, they gave little insight into their true personality. She recalled a couple of women who stood out.

Veronica wants a relationship with someone she can trust. Her admission that she's held back in the past and her regret about not telling someone how much he meant to her shows she's willing to be vulnerable. When Veronica shared that she thought she'd met the love of her life and he hurt her by leaving, Lanie couldn't help but feel a tinge of guilt because of what she'd done to James. It also inspired her to find the perfect guy for Veronica.

Also, that Jenna was something—so spirited and independent. Only a true partnership would do for her. She'll need someone driven and clear with his objectives, a man who isn't intimidated by a strong woman. Jenna knows what she wants and what she doesn't. Lanie felt akin to her after she shared that her biggest fear was losing her independence and the investment she's put into her career, having to trade it for marriage, or worse, that she won't give love a chance. Lanie knew Jenna needed a nudge to see what was right in front of her and she was thrilled to facilitate a match.

Now all she needed were two ideal men.

⸺

MEANWHILE, Ryan did some tallying of his own. He concluded that most of the guys were bores, with only a couple of exceptions. He really hit it off with a kid named

Parker, a thirty-something construction foreman with a lot of drive and an earnest heart. He liked his response about his favorite holiday and how it tied into his family's cabin in the mountains. He'll need someone who likes the outdoors and can handle large family gatherings.

Then there was Cameron. Still longing after he let the woman of his dreams get away. That guy poured it all out when he shared his story. It made him feel sorry for the dude. Ryan acknowledged he might have some residual guilt after abducting Lanie from her ex, but you know the saying. Still, it would be good penance if he could find Cameron the perfect girl, someone sweet and in it for the long run, someone he could make it up to, metaphorically, of course.

▭

"ROUND TWO," Shelly announced from the doorway to the room and two fresh faces marched in.

Lanie smiled from her chair as a handsome man in his late thirties approached. His dark brown hair and eyes stood out against his fair skin.

"Hello, I'm Cameron." His voice was deep and his eye contact uninterrupted.

"It's nice to meet you, Cameron. I have a few questions for you."

"Fire away," he replied.

"Describe your perfect Sunday with your significant other."

His eyes went downcast as he replied, "It's been a long while since I had a perfect Sunday. There was this one time when my old girlfriend and I, we just left the house on foot and let the day take us. We walked eight miles that day, stopped for coffee, lunch, and eventually drinks. After a few rounds of cocktails, we were done with the walking. We took a cab back to my place. Though it was only six in the evening, we went straight to bed and we stayed there until we had to leave for work the next day."

Lanie felt his longing for that moment and who could blame him? It sounded ideal. His answer made her want to go off script to learn why the relationship ended, but she stayed the course. "Thank you for your answer. May I ask, what is your biggest fear?"

He inhaled and looked Lanie right in the eye. "That I've already lost the best woman I'll ever know and nothing will be as good again."

Lanie could hold back no more and anyway, her question loosely followed the list. "Did she hurt you then?"

His sullen expression made her wonder if she'd pushed too far. "I hurt her and I'm sorry for it."

"Time's up. Next contestants, approach," Shelly called.

Lanie straightened her shoulders and tried to refocus as Cameron's words haunted her.

———

RYAN TOOK a sip of his water as his next interview, a tiny brunette with luscious curves called Veronica sat across from him. "Hi there," she blushed.

"Hello," Ryan replied. "Since we have only a few minutes, I'll start in with the questions."

"Okay," she smiled showing off her perfect white teeth and full red lips.

He cleared his throat, "What is the most embarrassing thing you've ever done?"

Veronica's smile melted as she stared at the table. "I tracked down my ex-boyfriend. He left for Los Angeles, said he was going for a job, but his ex was living there and

I knew they were talking. I didn't understand. I thought we had something special. So, I got on a plane and flew into town. When I got to his house, I saw them through the window. They looked so happy," she inhaled, "so I left."

As Ryan listened, his guts twisted and his mind snapped back in time to a similar moment in he and Lanie's journey. He knew he'd never forget that night on the roof. When he saw her holding hands with another man, it was devastating and humiliating. He and Veronica had one thing in common. They knew how it felt to lose love. Ryan was sure that with the right match she would find it again.

He scribbled some notes, more as a distraction, and wondered how he'd been chosen to match couples. "One more question: What was your favorite holiday memory?"

Veronica appeared to turn the question over and finally said, "Well, I was raised by my aunt as a single mother, so our holidays were kind of small, but there was this one day, it was my birthday, only my boyfriend didn't know. We'd only been dating a few weeks and I didn't want to put pressure on things, but the day worked out perfectly. We literally took a walk. We walked and talked all day and had a great time. When we got back, we spent the afternoon and all night in bed. It was the best birthday I've ever had.

Her answer struck Ryan as he'd heard something similar earlier in the night. His heart opened to this woman who asked for little and had been hurt. He wanted to help her and he had just the guy in mind…

⸻

A TALL, fit young man with clear blue eyes strode to Lanie's table. With an easy smile he said, "Hello, I'm Parker. How are you tonight?"

Lanie liked the dimples in his cheeks and his straw brown hair. He had a nice way about him. "I'm well. You happen to be my last interview."

He nodded, "I know. Thank you for meeting me."

"You're welcome. Shall we get started?"

"Sounds good," he replied.

"What is your biggest fear?"

Parker blinked and after a beat replied, "I'm afraid I won't meet my match. I know this sounds dumb, but I'm 36 and I still haven't found someone I could imagine spending my life with."

Lanie didn't think as she asked, "What kind of person are you looking for?"

"Hmm." He leaned back slightly and scratched his smooth chin. "She'd have to be smart, independent, and not afraid to stand up for what she believes in. Someone who loves family and snow sports, if that's not too much to ask." He laughed then.

She made a note and asked, "What's your idea of a perfect Sunday with your girlfriend?"

Parker tilted his head and shrugged, "Perfect would be she and I in the mountains. My family has a cabin and I've had a lot of great times there. It would be the best to finally share it with a woman I love."

Lanie blushed inwardly and thought it ludicrous that she was his matchmaker. "What if you met the love of your life and they hurt you? How would you handle that?"

He took a deep breath and said, "I'd try to understand what happened and why they did it. If watching my parents has taught me anything, it's that people make mistakes, and sometimes their mistakes cause pain. It's important to say you're sorry and mean it and just as important to accept an apology."

Lanie wasn't sure she was qualified for the task of

finding him love. If anything, Parker was giving her words of wisdom.

—

RYAN STIFLED a yawn as a lanky blonde with cornflower blue eyes approached his table. She sat and said, "Hello, I'm Jenna."

"Hi, Jenna. It's nice to meet you."

"You as well."

Ryan noticed she replied almost professionally. "Let's get started," he said.

"All right."

"Tell me about your best holiday memory."

She smiled sweetly and Ryan got a glimpse of her personality as she shared, "I have a big extended family and it's hard for us to fit into one place. A few years ago, we rented four neighboring houses in the mountains and had our own family compound over Thanksgiving weekend. It was the best time. We played in the snow, hung out late in the hot tub, and some of us went skiing or snowshoeing. Dinner was a moving party. We had a blast."

"That does sound fun," Ryan agreed. "Now, can you tell me, what's one decision you've made that you'd like to go back and change?"

She looked to the ceiling, huffed her bangs out of her face and announced, "I'd go to prom."

So what if a follow-up wasn't on the list? "You didn't go to your prom?"

"I didn't. I was too wrapped up in finishing senior year with perfect grades, and I was taking a few college courses to get a head start—but I don't know why I use that as the excuse for my not going. It was only one night. I could have spared it."

"Then why didn't you go?"

"There wasn't anyone to take me. Boys didn't like me much in school." She sniffed, "For that matter, they don't seem to like me much now. If I had it to do again, I'd go even without a date."

Looking at her, Ryan found her story hard to believe, but he could tell it wasn't faux modesty. This woman didn't know how stunning she was, nor how intimidating to the opposite sex. She was more than a complete package and not a lot of guys could stand beside her. But she didn't need a lot of guys, she just needed one, and he had someone in mind.

———

VERONICA AND JENNA held their champagne flutes up as Veronica toasted, "Here's to following through, no matter what."

Clink, the two friends tapped their glasses and Jenna said, "Cheers."

A gulp or two later, Jenna ventured, "How do you really feel?"

Veronica shook her head and said, "Way too sober. One more?"

Jenna nodded, "Yes," and followed her petite pal through the crowd as she headed for the bar. Veronica made her presence known and set about ordering another round while Jenna scanned the crowd.

"Oh no." She whispered as her co-worker Parker Jones approached.

His cheeks were flushed and his smile almost maniacal. "Wow, Jenna. You're here," he stated awkwardly.

"Yes, I am," she replied, "and so are you. Weird."

"Unexpected," he replied.

"You certainly are," chimed Veronica from their elbow height.

Jenna looked down. "Parker, this is my best friend Veronica. Veronica, meet Parker. He and I work together."

"Nice to meet you, Parker." Veronica smiled devilishly toward her friend. "So this is the Parker you've told me about." She looked him up and down, adding, "Seems you left out a few things."

Jenna squirmed against Parker's stare as he asked, "You told her about me? What did you say?"

Veronica didn't hold back. "She called you infuriating and smart, but annoyingly so."

Parker smirked, "Hmm. So, you think I'm smart?"

Jenna shook her head. "That's what you gleaned from her comment. You know you're smart."

Parker's eyes pinned Jenna. "Not as smart as you."

Jenna had to flee the awkward moment. "Well, if you'll excuse us, we're going to run to the restroom. Maybe I'll see you later or at work next week."

Hands in his pockets, he tipped back on his heels and said, "It was good to see you, Jenna."

She practically ran to the restroom with Veronica trailing behind. They made it inside and were waiting their turn when Veronica asked, "Why didn't you tell me that the Parker you've been complaining about was so hot?"

"Is he?" Jenna's voice raised an octave as she replied.

"You know he is."

"Honestly, I don't think of him that way. We're co-workers and I work with mostly men. I don't spend my days thinking about if they're good-looking or not."

"Well that explains why you need this, but what about me?"

"You are still hung up on your ex and you know it."

"Hold that thought," Veronica said as she scurried into an open stall.

———

AFTER A QUICK LOOK in the mirror, the women were ready to return to the party. They knew their chances of being paired were slim so they decided to get drunk and mingle. A server approached with a tray of champagne.

"Oh yes," cheered Veronica as she took two flutes, handing one to Jenna. Before they could take a sip, Veronica felt a tap on her shoulder and Jenna's eyes grew into saucers. Veronica turned to see who it was and nearly dropped her glass when she found herself facing her ex—the one that got away—Cameron. She was frozen.

"V, it's amazing to see you." His expression was awestruck. "I can't believe it."

Since Veronica was still at a loss for words, Jenna chimed in, "Hey, Cameron, remember me?"

"Oh wow, Jenna," he exclaimed. "I'm glad you girls are still friends."

Jenna didn't know how to feel. She had so many questions, things she wanted to know, and she found she still wanted to kick his ass after what he had done to her friend five years ago.

Veronica finally found her voice, "Well, it was something bumping into you. We're headed to the ladies' room. I...I'll see you." She rushed to the safety of the restroom with Jenna closely trailing.

Once inside Jenna said what Veronica was thinking. "Holy crap! First, I bump into a co-worker and now you run into Cameron. How are you feeling? Are you okay?"

Veronica was reeling and she said as much. "I'm shocked. To see him again after all these years—in this way

—what are the chances? What he did when he left, I was crushed and it still hurts. I don't know what to think about us crossing paths again, and like this."

Jenna shook her head. "What do you want to do? We can leave. We don't have to stay until the announcement. It won't be us anyway."

Veronica squared her shoulders and met Jenna's gaze. "No, we can't leave. We made a pact to see it through until the end. We have to stay until the announcements and we'll accept whatever comes our way."

Jenna bit her lower lip and weighed Veronica's words against her own good judgement. Throwing caution to the wind, she said, "I'm still in."

"Me too. Let's go."

⬜

"GOOD EVENING, WWW.LOVETEST.LOVE CONTESTANTS." *Tap, tap, tap,* Shelly brought the room to attention. "It's been a fun night so far and we're not done yet. The results are being tabulated and we'll soon announce the ultimate matches for tonight's event. Now is the perfect time to mingle and to get to know the highly compatible singles in the room. Cheers, everybody."

"Cheers," the room erupted.

⬜

LANIE'S blonde curls dangled temptingly along her cheek, distracting Ryan from the task at hand of reading her interview notes. He'd already made up his mind, so he skipped to his favorites to see if their picks synced. A smile came to his face as he viewed her notes on Veronica. Cameron's name was written in the corner and underlined twice. *Check*, he thought to himself and quickly scanned the profile for Jenna. They were two for two as she confirmed his guess by writing Parker's name with the words independent and family.

He looked up from the pages in time to catch her watching him. "Hello there," he drawled.

"Husband."

Her voice and those words sent chills down his spine. "Wife."

"I like your notes. Would you say your top couples are Veronica and Cameron and Jenna and Parker?"

His nose crinkled as he chuckled. "Well, given my vast experience in matchmaking and superior training on the subject, yes. Veronica and Cameron and Jenna and Parker seemed to make the most sense to me. Do you agree?"

"I do."

More chills as he realized the goddess in green was his forever. "You're stunning."

Her eyes didn't break and her voice was a caress. "Thank you."

"Knock, knock," the subtle Shelly broke into the room. "Are your choices narrowed?"

"They are," Ryan answered. "We pick: Veronica & Cameron and Jenna & Parker."

She took their notes and said, "Perfect. You've got about fifteen minutes before the award. I'll see you out there."

Ryan stood and, without hesitation, took Lanie's hand. "We'd better hurry. I've got something to do and you'll want to pop into the ladies before we announce the winners."

She should have been embarrassed by him noticing her already weakening bladder, but she found it sweet and comforting. Also, she was intrigued as to where they were going. Lanie was all for a quickie, but this seemed a bit extreme considering the function that was going on. It didn't take long for her to figure out his plan as he pulled her toward the very spot where they first bumped into one another.

It all came rushing back to her. The frenzied nerves she felt as she scanned the lobby and saw no sign of her best friend Audrey. Digging through her handbag and then running right into Ryan. His eyes seemed to know her and she felt something click as he righted her. She wasn't free when they met, but their paths crossed and she opened up to another possibility. If any one thing had gone differently that day, she and Ryan would never have met and they would have missed so much.

He stopped to face her and, holding her close, said, "Meeting you was the best thing that ever happened to me. Had you been a minute later or if you hadn't accepted that dare, we wouldn't be here now. I don't know what to believe about destiny, but I want you to know I'm grateful for every step that led us here. I still can't believe you chose me. I love you."

"I love you, Ryan."

His kiss was tender, painfully so. A few passersby whistled and others clapped, causing them to break apart. Lanie smiled into the eyes of her man as he placed an arm around her shoulders and they walked toward the stage.

———

VERONICA TUGGED on Jenna's arm. "Look, they're heading to the front. Shall we get a spot?"

Jenna glanced half-heartedly at Jack, the engineer she'd been speaking with—"Excuse us, Jack. We'll see you later"—and she followed Veronica toward the front of the room.

"Exciting, huh?" Veronica's tone and expression seemed forced.

"Are you okay?"

"Sure, sure. It's just, I saw Cameron and I wanted to get…"

Cameron arrived at her side. "Hi again."

"Oh, hey," she managed.

Jenna was distracted by a tap at her shoulder and when she turned Parker was standing there looking a bit lost. "Hi again."

"Parker," she said simply.

"Ladies and gentlemen, gather around. I'm Shelly, your www.lovetest.love event coordinator. How is everyone doing tonight?"

The room erupted in cheers, yet Veronica and Jenna remained quiet.

"Are you ready for the big announcement?"

Another explosion of excitement vibrated from the audience.

"Put your hands together as we're joined by Ryan and Lanie Glass, the King and Queen of www.lovetest.love.

Lanie and Ryan took the stage and Ryan started. "First, let me just say how fun it was to meet with everyone. I loved the stories you shared and really appreciate you trusting us to weigh in on your ideal romantic partner. I'm completely unqualified for the task, but what I've learned about love is if it's true, it finds a way."

He stepped back as catcalls echoed in the room. Lanie began, "Everyone who knows me knows I was against online dating. I'd never tried it until I heard about the www.lovetest.love approach. While it wasn't their algorithm that brought me to Ryan, if I hadn't done something completely out of character, I would have missed out on the most incredible man I've ever known. Congratulations on being here and for taking the first step in your journey to love."

Whistles and clapping greeted them as they each picked up an envelope. Ryan said to Lanie, "Ladies first."

She tore open the envelope and her eyes lit up. "The first couple who was paired by the algorithm and coincidentally Ryan and I is Cameron and Veronica. Where are they? Come up, Veronica and Cameron."

Jenna knocked Veronica in the shoulder. Their eyes met as Cameron took Veronica's hand and led her to the stage. Ryan shook Cameron's hand and Lanie hugged Veronica as they joined them on the platform.

Ryan raised his hand, "Quiet, let's get the second couple up here." He tore into the envelope and his face beamed, "Our second couple that was paired by the algorithm and Lanie and I is Jenna and Parker. Come on up, kids."

Parker placed an arm around Jenna as she tried to dig in. With a minor push, he got her moving toward the stage. They greeted their hosts and the other couple and as Lanie and Ryan took over the announcement, Jenna and Veronica shared an incredulous look between them.

Ryan asked, "Isn't this exciting, everyone? These exquisitely matched couples have won five incredible date experiences and we get to follow their progress with interviews after each one and a broadcasted finale. The night isn't over yet. There's plenty of time to make your own match."

Lanie grabbed the mic, "Make love, everyone! We intend to." Ryan swooped her up and stormed off the stage. They left the room in a trail of applause.

SHELLY PULLED the newly minted couples into the interview room, "Congratulations, everyone."

They stood awkwardly.

"I want to remind you of the process and rules as we get started. We'll email you a schedule with days to block off for your dates. Ryan Glass will interview you the day after each event and his schedule will alternate between the men and the women. As for communication or meetings, outside of the planned excursions, that is strictly prohibited. Now that we've used technology to get us most of the way, we want the part of you getting to know one another to be as personal as possible. The dates are designed with plenty of opportunity for face to face communication. We want to deter anything further until after the decision on Valentine's Day. We feel our process will give you the space to reflect as well as the needed time to build a strong foundation."

"Um, excuse me," Jenna hesitated.

"Yes, Jenna?"

"Well, there's a little problem with Parker and I."

Shelly's eyebrows rose, "Oh?"

"You see, we know each other, from work. We work for the same company."

Shelly replied, "Oh."

"And," Veronica chimed in while pointing to Cameron, "we also know each other. We dated five years ago."

Shelly repeated, "Oh." After a beat she said, "Give me a minute," and scurried from the room, leaving the lucky contestants in an awkward state.

Veronica was the first one to crack. She started laughing and they all stared her way. When she didn't stop,

Parker took one look at Jenna and he joined in. Soon all four of them were giggling.

Jenna had tears streaming down her face but eventually managed, "Guys, what are we going to do?"

Cameron's eyes met Veronica's and no one had time to reply before Shelly whistled to announce her return, silencing their laughter.

She came to stand before them. Her was expression stern as she said, "It is funny and the tech's agreed. We're going with it. We're going with it but the rules are amended."

"Jenna and Parker, if you have to talk to each other at work, so be it, but nothing beyond that. No co-worker lunches, no texts, emails, nada. Do you agree?"

Her assumptive stance left no room for debate. They looked at one another. Parker shrugged in challenge and Jenna met his nonchalance. "Agreed," they said at once.

"Veronica and Cameron, the same rules apply to you. No texts, emails, phone calls, or dates outside of the schedule until after Valentine's Day."

They nodded in agreement, knowing they'd just committed to opening old wounds, but what were the odds they'd find one another again and in this way?

"Well, kids, that's it for me. Say your goodbyes until you meet again in two weeks…" Shelly exited the room and they knew things were about to get interesting.

4

DATE #1 (The Saturday Before Thanksgiving)

Jenna paced the living room nervously as Veronica primped in the floor to ceiling mirror. "Sit down, crazy. You're wearing a groove in that rug."

Jenna snapped her head in Veronica's direction and with a look of terror in her eyes, she said, "What have I agreed to?

Veronica took a focused breath in and out before replying. "What have WE agreed to?"

"Yeah, that!" Jenna fired.

"We agreed to see it through. Trust me, I'm not feeling great about this either. The guy who dumped me, the one I've never quite gotten over, is somehow my ideal match. It's sad to believe that the best guy for me is the one who already left me."

Jenna hadn't thought of it from that vantage point and she tried to console her closest friend. "Well, he didn't seem too upset about it. In fact, he was the one who came up to you first. Maybe he regrets what happened between you."

Veronica looked suspicious and her tone matched.

"Maybe. And listen, you and Parker aren't doing anything wrong. It's not a big deal to hang out with a co-worker or even date him. You should just have fun."

"It's not that simple, Veronica. I work with mostly men. If they find out about Parker and me, their whispers and assumptions will actually have merit."

"What assumptions? That you're dating and you met him at work? Who cares? All you ever do is work. Where else would you meet someone?"

"You don't understand how construction is. People like to talk. This will affect my career, trust me."

A knock at the door interrupted their freak-out session and Veronica went to answer. Cameron waited on the other side. "Good morning," he said. "You look beautiful."

Veronica tried for neutrality as her heart skipped a beat. He looked so handsome in the navy sweater and black jeans he wore. "Good morning. Let me get my purse."

"Okay." He peeked through the open door and called, "Hello again, Jenna."

"Hey, Cameron. Don't mess it up this time."

Her firm directive had him standing a little taller. "I won't."

Veronica returned wearing her black hooded trench and said, "Shall we?"

"Let's go," he agreed and they waved goodbye to Jenna.

━

ALONE WITH HER OWN THOUGHTS, Jenna admitted to herself that she was terrified to be one on one with Parker. She had no idea what they would talk about or how to address the elephant in the room—they both agreed to be matched when there is an obvious work conflict. She didn't have long to ponder before a knock at the door signified his arrival.

Jenna put on her best poker face and opened the door.

"Hi, Jenna."

She tried for levity, and to ignore how sexy he looked in his dark Levi's and black leather jacket. "Hey, Parker, it's been a while."

He laughed, "Well, it's nice to see you outside of meetings."

"Thanks," she replied. "Should we go?"

"Sure, I don't know where to, but we've got a hell of a ride and a bottle of champagne waiting for us."

Jenna walked outside to find a limo and she had to laugh, "So much for discreet."

———

CAMERON HANDED Veronica a glass of champagne as they made their way onto the highway. The partition between them and the driver was closed and with their privacy came an awkwardness that only the bubbles would erase.

"Thank you," she managed.

He tapped his glass to hers, "Here's to the surprise of seeing you again."

Veronica said nothing, but took a sip.

He continued, unaffected, "What are the odds, right?"

She nodded and took another sip of her champagne. After a period of silence, she blurted, "What happened to Kyra?"

Cameron looked as if he'd been slapped. "We didn't work out. Umm, after I moved to LA we gave it a try, but things just didn't feel right anymore, for either of us."

"When did you move back to Oregon?"

"Not even a year later. I missed everything about being here. LA wasn't for me."

Veronica absorbed his words and also what he didn't say. For example, how he never felt compelled to get back in touch with her. *I guess he didn't miss everything.*

They rode in silence for a while until Cameron asked, "How's your Aunt Jasmine these days?"

Veronica smiled as she thought of her hippie leaning Aunt-Mom. "She's good. You won't believe it but she's married. To a woman of course. Her name is Glenda. They've converted the house to solar electric and their cars. She finally found her person."

"That's great to hear. She's a fun person, so positive."

"Yeah, she is something else."

They drove in silence for a while, each to their own thoughts. The grey sky cast shadows through the sunroof's glass and as they finished their wine, Veronica tried to understand why this was happening. Why were they matched? And why did she agree to go on five dates with a man who dumped her and never spoke to her again?

He ventured, "How's work going? Are you still teaching second grade?"

She nodded, "Caught me. I am. I know I should be more ambitious, but I love teaching kids and second grade is my favorite. What about you? Did you stay in finance?"

He shook his head, "No actually. I moved into commercial real estate. It's been interesting and a good move. And I think being a teacher is ambitious. I couldn't do it."

The divider suddenly rolled down as their driver announced, "We are close to our destination. You may want to check out the view as we make our final few turns."

They pulled off the highway and followed a narrow road up the side of a steep hillside. It felt as if they were engulfed by towering evergreens and the golden yellow leaves that exploded from the elderly Garry oaks. A dilapidated barn rotted in the distance while a solitary horse grazed out front. Another turn and a few farm stands could be seen. Pumpkins and gourds were available for purchase at the roadside stands.

The road narrowed and they entered a narrow bridge that warned of one-way traffic only. It made sense because the bridge was scarcely wide enough for one vehicle, let alone passing. The carved rock pillars were arranged perfectly until every once in a while, a gap could be found —evidence that the century old bridge had seen better days. They pulled up to the Vista House and the driver selected a spot closest to the entry.

The limo door opened and Cameron stepped out first and held out a hand to help Veronica out. It was the first time they'd touched all day. "Would you like a picture before your lunch?"

The wind whipped up and Veronica's hair smothered Cameron. He laughed, "We would, only I'll move downwind."

They walked toward the rock wall and took in once what had to be one of the world's most incredible views. Evergreens soared above and below them and resided between the golden yellow leaves of ancient oaks. The Columbia river seemed to jut from a jagged cliff. It encircled the island and divided the lands between Washington and Oregon with its deep blue waters and frigid wake. The air was icy and the sun bright.

As Veronica studied the view, she felt Cameron's eyes on her. "You look beautiful today, Veronica."

She looked down at her black jeans and white off the

shoulder sweater with an uncomfortable shrug. He moved to her side and turned her around so their back was to the view. "We're ready for our picture now," he called to their driver, John.

"Perfect spot. Okay, you two, on the count of three, say cheese. One, two, three..."

"Cheese," they said, though they felt silly.

"Excellent, I got a few. I'm sure you'll like one of them. Are you ready for your lunch?"

They looked at each other and John. "Sure," Cameron agreed for the both of them.

"This way," he said and they made their way up the marble stairs and into the gothic building. "You will be dining in the jewel of the crown, so to speak." They followed him up a curved stairway until they arrived at the top. John removed a key from his pocket and unlocked the only door, "Through here."

The corridor was pitch dark except a spotlight that brightened the floor at the end of the narrow passage. John walked ahead, Veronica followed, and Cameron brought up the rear. As they turned the corner, the world became emerald. Through the vintage glass, they saw a 180-degree view of the forest and rushing river.

Veronica surveyed the space. Brocade rugs and aged leather furnishings rested against a heavenly backdrop. No traditional Northwest respite would be complete without the requisite buck mounted on the wall, or the wood-burning fire that crackled softly beneath it. At the widest window was a table set for two. Silver dishware and matching goblets rested against white linen.

John directed, "Before I leave, let me tell you a few things about the room. There's a restroom through there." He pointed past a bookshelf. "Your lunch will be served in thirty minutes and until then there are a couple of bottles of wine and some snacks at the buffet." He waved toward an antique cabinet along the wall. "Later there will be dessert. You may have noticed there are also board games, books, and a cozy fire to keep you entertained. I will return in three hours. Have fun."

Three hours, Veronica panicked silently. What the hell are we going to talk about for three hours?

"Thank you, John. We'll see you later," Cameron answered as the driver escaped. He turned toward Veronica. "Wine?"

"Absolutely," she agreed.

He crossed the room and poured two glasses. "It's a Washington Pinot." He said as Veronica approached. "Here you go."

"Thank you."

He tapped his glass to hers and they both took a sip. "Do you want to sit?" he asked.

"Sure." She turned and looked at the options. The deep sofa with the thick white blanket draped over the arm looked too comfortable. The game table chairs looked a bit stiff, perfect. "How about over there?"

Cameron followed her across the room to the game table. Taking the seat opposite her, he joked, "Perfect, let's sit at the game table. If I bore you, I'll have backup."

She sipped her wine and didn't reply. "Wow, it's gorgeous out today," he commented. "Hey, look, look over there."

His voice was excited and Veronica had to see what caused it. "Oh my." She replied and they watched a red-tailed hawk soar along the tree line above the water.

"This place really is a gem. Who knew this was up here?"

She sipped her wine and nodded, "Agreed. I've been here on field trips, but we never got to see this room."

"Do you want any snacks?" Cameron asked and jumped to his feet.

"Sure," she replied to his beautiful backside. She had to admit, he was still as handsome as ever, with his thick dark hair and almost black eyes. The past five years had treated him well. She even admired the tiny crow's feet that were beginning to form at his eyes.

He returned with a cutting board upon which were slices of brie, pear, and assorted salami. "That looks great."

He kidded, "Well, I hope you like it because I slaved all day."

She plucked a slice of pear from the plate and topped it with cheese. "This is awkward."

He nodded, "Agreed. I'm sorry."

She decided it was time to address it head on: "Why are you here?"

Cameron swirled the wine in his glass. "Are you asking why I went on the matchmaking app or why I agreed to do this process with you?"

Without hesitation she said, "Yes and yes."

"Are you sure you want to know the answer?"

"I want to know."

"I went on the matchmaking site to meet someone— hopefully *the* someone I'm meant to be with."

Her voice was near toneless. "Then I'm even more confused why you agreed to do this with me."

Cameron set his glass aside and he took her hand in his. "I agreed to do this with you because I've never forgotten a single moment we shared. I know I messed up and I won't blame you if you can't forgive me, but I won't forgive myself if I don't find out if what we had is still there."

Veronica pulled her hand from his and rose to walk across the room. Her back was turned and silence weighted the space. "Good afternoon," called a cheerful woman who carried a tray. "I've got lunch for you."

"Oh, thank you," said Cameron.

Veronica turned and watched the woman set covered plates on the table. She removed the lids and announced, "Local salmon, greens, and sautéed potatoes. Enjoy lunch, you two."

"It looks wonderful, thank you," Veronica called.

"You're welcome. I'll bring dessert in shortly."

Cameron walked over to the chair and pulled it out, "Veronica."

"Thanks," she said and took her seat.

He went for the bottle of wine then joined her at the table. With their glasses filled he said, "Here's to my great fortune of sharing another day with you."

Veronica took a sip of her wine and replaced the glass on the table. She knew she needed to turn the other cheek, at least for the moment. "Tell me about your job. What's involved in commercial real estate?"

He buttered a piece of bread and said, "I do a few things. I'm work with some investment groups, I lease commercial space, and I sell land or buildings to developers. I'm a partner at the company. We're not large by any stretch but we've got a strong presence in the Northwest."

"That sounds very grown up."

"I am grown up. It took a while. How do you like the salmon?"

"Yeah, it's good."

He shook his head, "You don't have to be polite for me. I remember it's not your favorite."

"It's okay. I've come around. Do you still cook?"

"I do, and what's more, now I can afford the ingredients."

She laughed, "Hey, don't knock the improv that comes

from bare cupboards. Chips Ahoy scrambled eggs are still my guilty pleasure."

He laughed, "I forgot about that. Why didn't we just go to the store?" There was an awkward silence as they both recalled that stormy night at his apartment on Alberta. They were so in love they couldn't bear to leave the bedroom, let alone the house. That's when they first developed the chocolate chip cookie scramble. "Oh, yeah."

Veronica took a swig of her wine and changed the subject. "So, how are your parents?"

"They're good, really good. I saw mom yesterday for lunch. She was thrilled to hear we matched."

"You told you mother? She remembers me?"

"This may sound familiar, but yes and yes. Why wouldn't she remember you? We dated for nearly a year."

"I know but it was five years ago and…"

"She remembers you. Actually, she's never stopped reminding me about you."

Veronica was dying to know more but she wouldn't give him the satisfaction of asking. Fortunately, she was saved by the arrival of dessert.

The woman sang more than asked, "How is your lunch?"

"Very good," Cameron replied.

"Great, thank you," said Veronica.

"I hope you like double chocolate cake and coffee because that's dessert."

Cameron answered, "You're talking to the right people."

They sat silently as she cleared the plates and replaced them with dessert. After she filled each coffee cup, she placed a carafe of cream between them. "Enjoy the rest of your afternoon, you two."

"Thank you," they chimed.

After she left, Cameron ventured, "Want to sit on the couch, maybe play a game of cards?"

"How about Scrabble?" she challenged.

"Aww, okay. My defeat is imminent."

"Well, we wouldn't want to damage your precious ego."

"Hey, I was just kidding."

"I know, but I wasn't. I'm trying not to be pissed at you, but it's not easy."

"I get that." He stood and walked toward the bookshelf and a moment later returned with the Scrabble board. "Shall we?"

"Sure thing. I'll pop into the restroom and when I come back, prepare to get smacked down."

He nodded amiably. "I'll be ready."

When she returned, they picked up the game as they picked up their relationship. Years later, they still had something and if it took a prop like Scrabble to inch them forward and also back, it was well worth it. Time passed quickly as they competed and covered the board with letters.

Soon John arrived. "Hello, Cameron and Veronica. It's time to leave. I'll meet you at the car in five minutes."

"Okay, we'll be right down."

Cameron looked at Veronica. Her cheeks were flushed from the wine and coffee and her features at ease. "This was so much fun. Thank you for giving it a try."

She could feel her resolve weakening. A war waged between her feminist side and the woman who once loved the man who faced her. "It was a date, no big deal. I had fun too."

If her neutral comment deterred him, Cameron took it in stride. They made their way downstairs and into the limo. On ride back into town the mood was subdued. They spoke little but the quiet wasn't awkward. They'd touched on a lot for a first date and even more because of their history.

As they neared her house Cameron said, "I know we can't talk until our next date, but I want you to know, I wish we could. I'm really excited we found each other again."

For years she longed to hear those words, to know he wanted her as she wanted him. It was both thrilling and terrifying to find herself with him again. She had to tell him the truth. "I'll admit, it is a coincidence that we found ourselves matched, but I'm not making you any promises. I may not be able to get past what's already happened."

"The only thing that matters is there's hope, Veronica. I just want to see you again."

They pulled to a stop at her house and John was quick to open the car door. "There's no need to walk me up. I'll see you on our next date, Cameron."

He smiled so sweetly it almost hurt her, "I'm looking forward to it, Veronica."

⸺

PARKER HANDED a glass of bubbles to Jenna and raised his in toast. "Here's to getting out of the office. Not that I spend a lot of time in the office, but, well…you know what I mean."

His clumsy toast put Jenna at ease. "Cheers," she laughed and sipped the crisp wine.

Parker took a drink as well and managed to get it down the front of his sweater. He quickly brushed it off as if nothing had happened and Jenna had to look out the window to spare him the embarrassment.

"Looks like we're heading toward the wine country," said Jenna.

He ducked his head to peek out the window. "Sure does."

His cologne was spicy, like cardamom and burnt orange, and his fine hair was a bit mussed. Jenna knew this was a disaster waiting to happen. If she were conducting a safety survey, this scenario would have a long list of infractions.

"Do you like wine?" he asked.

"I do. I actually grew up next door to a winery in Yamhill. My childhood included a heavy dose of playing hide and seek in the vines with the neighbor kids."

"That sounds great."

"Yeah, it was. What about you? Where did you grow up?"

"We lived in Camas. I moved to Portland after school."

"Nice. Do you have a lot of family around here?"

He laughed then, and it was the first time he seemed relaxed since the date began. "I do. My parents still live in Washington. My immediate family is a brother and two sisters. I'm the baby. Everyone else is married and I have two nieces and three nephews. Plus, a slew of aunts, uncles, and cousins. And you?"

"It's just me and my brother for immediate family and my parents are still in the house in Yamhill. I do have a dozen aunts and uncles though and more cousins than I can count. I'm not an aunt yet which is a good thing since my brother is only seventeen."

"Wow, that's a pretty big gap between kids."

"Yeah, sixteen years. My poor parents had to start all over again. Kind of funny too. They rolled with it like champs though and my little brother is pretty cool."

The driver turned up a gravel road, the wheels

crunched as they made it to the top. A wood and glass building flanked the entry as they turned down the cobble-stone road and parked. Their driver, Bryce, circled around the car to open the door.

Jenna got out first, taking Bryce's hand to assist and Parker quickly followed. "Wow," he exclaimed. "This is gorgeous."

Jenna wandered to the edge of the hill and called, "Isn't it?"

He joined her and Bryce said, "Let me get a picture of you. It's a great spot with the vines and that mountain behind you."

They looked at one another then turned his direction. "Get closer," he called.

Parker put his arm around Jenna's back and she nearly bristled. "Now say wine," Bryce teased.

"Wine," they said at once.

"Excellent. Let's get you situated, shall we?"

They followed Bryce through the parking lot and toward the main building. A small courtyard with hiber-nating bushes and plants decorated the gravel and slate path. Soon they found themselves upon a terrace that appeared to jut out into the unfolding golden hillsides. With a glass wall and a steep drop, the dramatic design left them on the edge.

"Pretty, isn't it?" Bryce said. "If you'll come this way, I think you'll like what's in store."

Parker shrugged happily and they followed him into a building that was composed of steel and glass. The terrace fed into a glorious tasting room with a wide oak counter and a smattering of cocktail tables. Everywhere they looked the vines seemed to follow. "We're through here," said Bryce, who opened a door at the end of the hall and they entered a private tasting room. A table and chairs looked to be floating by a wall of windows, emphasizing the steel sky and recently harvested vines.

To the side was a fireplace were a leather couch and a coffee table, upon which was a plate of assorted cheeses and charcuterie. Bryce inquired, "What do you think?"

"Wow. This is all for us?" Parker asked.

"For the next three hours it is. Let me show you a couple of things. There's an assortment of wine on the bar cart," he waved. "Snacks are here to tide you over until lunch is served. It should be here in about thirty minutes. Oh, and one more thing." He crossed the room to a sliding door, "This is your private and heated balcony. Feel free to take your dessert here."

"This is very nice, Bryce. Thank you."

"No thanks are needed. Enjoy your afternoon." And he vanished through the door, leaving them to their tasting suite.

"This is almost too good to be true." Jenna said.

Parker's eyes locked onto hers. "I was thinking the exact same thing." He felt the heat rise at his cheeks and redirected. "Wine?"

"Um, yes."

He went about pouring the first bottle. "This is a 2018 Pinot Noir from this vineyard." Handing a glass to Jenna, he said, "Here's to the good life."

"To the good life."

Parker asked, "Well, what should we do first? Sit by the fire? Survey the lands from our personal balcony?"

The fire did look cozy, but a little too intimate for the moment. "If you had box seats to a Seahawks game, would you rather wander the halls and watch on the monitor or would you use the seats? Let's check out the view."

His eyes grew wide, "So, you like football?"

She laughed and, glass in hand, made her way to the

door. The wind whipped as they stepped outside. The south-facing balcony overlooked the botanical garden and a dilapidated brick mansion on the opposing hill. The heat lamp glowed brightly, trying desperately to regulate the temperature against unpredictable wind gusts.

"Spectacular but breezy," said Parker.

Jenna was cold, but being outside was far less intimate and she needed that for now. "I guess we'll just have to warm up with our wine." She practically gulped it down.

"Want to sit?" Parker motioned toward two Adiron-dack chairs.

"Sure."

The wind was a little less as they huddled into their chairs. Jenna decided to dive into the deep end by addressing their work situation head on. "This is weird. Don't you think? We've been working together for how long?"

"Just over a year," he replied.

"My questions was rhetorical, but thank you. In over a year, we never considered each other this way. I'm not sure we should blow up our careers just because an algorithm thinks we're compatible."

He coughed, "Wait, who said anything about blowing up our careers? Why do you think that's going to happen?"

"Well, we'll be dating each other for a few months. We agreed to being interviewed by the newspaper. That means they're going to print this story. People will find out, especially if you tell them…"

"Me?" His tone was as crisp as the air and his stare direct. "Is that what you think? I'd kiss and tell?"

She sputtered, "I, I don't know. Maybe. Guys talk and if you haven't noticed I'm the only woman in project management. I'm not trying to whine, but it's already tough. How do you think they'll look at me if they think you and I are…together?"

Parker went quiet. He looked to the distant hillside then back at Jenna. "I like you. I always have, but I might never have asked you out if it weren't for the dating app and not because I didn't want to, because of what you just said. I know the guys would talk and I wouldn't like it."

Jenna reeled at his admission and she asked softly, "So, what do we do?"

Parker reached for Jenna's hand, "We date secretly until the decision and then we decide. By then, we'll know what to do."

His solution sounded simple, too simple, but Jenna liked the way his fingers caressed her palm and the ease he brought to the situation. For a moment, she was lost in his eyes. Were they blue or green? She couldn't tell…

"Hello." The sliding door opened. "I'm Lola and I've brought you lunch."

With the spell broken, they stood and made their way inside. "Thank you," replied Parker.

"Of course. I've set you up at the table. Brisket tacos are on the menu with a fresh bottle of wine. I'll bring in dessert in soon. Oh, and there's a coat rack over there," she pointed to a wall of hooks by the fireplace.

"Thank you so much, Lola," Jenna called after her retreating back.

Parker peeked at the table and said, "This looks awesome."

"It does," Jenna agreed and she placed her coat on the rack. As Parker hung his, she couldn't help but notice he had a nice backend, and he was tall—a fact that Jenna appreciated since she was 5' 7" and hated towering over her dates.

After they sat, Jenna touched Parker's hand, "Hey,

thank you for what you said before. It made a lot of sense. Hopefully we can keep work and," she waved her hand between them, "this separate."

"I'm sure we can." He raised his glass and Jenna joined.

Lunch was easier than expected. Plied by the wine and their newfound commonality that they both came from large families, there was plenty to discuss. Their pact to keep things between them–for now–created a bond of sorts.

"I've got dessert," Lola announced from the doorway.

Jenna protested. "I'm not sure we have room after those tacos. They were the best, by the way."

"Yes, they are. I bet you'll find space for this little sweet plate too. I'll put it here, by the fire."

"Thank you, Lola," Parker stood.

"Of course! Enjoy the chocolates. They are hand-made here in town."

Jenna stood too, "You should have led with chocolate. There's always room for a truffle or two."

Lola laughed and scurried out of the room.

"Hey, look at that!" Parker's eyes lit up as he stared out the window.

Jenna looked below. "Oh, wow, longhorns. They're beautiful."

They watched a herd of at least a dozen white cattle make their daily pilgrimage along the well-worn path. Single file, they marched, stopping occasionally to graze, but quickly resuming along a road they'd created with generations of shuffling hoofs.

Parker shook his head, "I could get used to this life."

"Me too. It's ideal."

"Want to sit by the fire?"

"Sure."

Despite her initial trepidation, Jenna found herself lulled into the date. She was starting to think of Parker as a man and not a co-worker. The shift might seem small to others, but for her it was big.

They sunk into the couch and he refilled their glasses. "Bottomless wine," he said as he handed hers over. Next, he picked up the plate of chocolate and offered it to her. "Something sweet?"

Jenna plucked a chocolate ball with green sprinkles from the plate and said, "Wonder what's inside?"

He watched her sniff and take a tentative bite. "Mmmm, it's out of this world."

"What is it?"

"You have to try," she said and foisted the remaining half his way.

His eyes flashed mischievously, and his mouth twitched as if he may bite it from her fingers, but his boldness was short lived as he gingerly took the chocolate from her fingers and popped it in his mouth. "Heavenly. What do you think, green tea and mint?"

"That's what I'd guess."

"Want to try another?" he goaded.

"Yes. You pick."

He scanned the options and landed on a white chocolate piece with red shavings on the top. "This one." He showed her. "You first."

"If you insist," she chided and took the candy and a dainty bite. "Mmm, no way. It's even better than the first."

She held it to his lips and he took it with less bravado than expected. His eyes closed as he delivered his review, "Roses, berry, and bourbon vanilla."

She practically purred, "So, so, good. Mind if I ask you a question?"

He laughed softly, "I think it's expected. Go for it."

"Why did you sign up for Love Test? You seem pretty normal and like you wouldn't have a hard time finding a date."

"Pretty normal?" He laughed, " I could say the same to you." His eyes held, "I'm not looking for *a* date. I'm looking for *the* date."

She was dying to know if today measured up to his *the* date quest, but she wouldn't ask. Instead, she took another piece of chocolate from the tray and held it to his mouth. They sat that way, eating rich chocolate paired with dark wine and they forgot they knew, but didn't know, one another. On that chill afternoon, they began to discover what the algorithm had already determined. They were compatible.

The fire glowed softly, casting warm light on Jenna's face. A strand of her long blonde hair fell across her cheek. With the lightest touch, Parker, tucked it behind her ear. Time froze and so did they, paused at the precipice of a kiss that might change everything. It seemed he had decided for both of them as he leaned closer...

"Oh darn, sorry to interrupt you two." Bryce entered the room and they hastened to their respective sides of the couch. Was that a smirk he tried to mask? "It's time to go. I'll see you out front in a few minutes."

"Okay, thanks, Bryce," Jenna replied and chuckled as he walked away.

Parker leaned in, "Busted."

She couldn't help but think about the real possibility of them being found. "See, we're no good at this already."

"I've been thinking about it. Let's ask them not to print our pictures in the article. I know the broadcast will be a thing, but we can deal with that when it comes."

"I agree with the part about no pictures, but sooner or

later this is going to come out. We should take things slow, just in case."

She didn't notice his crestfallen expression as he followed her to the car, but she did feel a chill run down her spine once they stepped away from their afternoon hideaway. The drive back was quiet. Jenna fought to stay awake as the wine caught up with her and Parker took in the scenery without comment.

They approached her house and pulled to a stop. Jenna turned to Parker. "It was a fun afternoon. I'll see you at work on Monday, where we won't be talking about this."

"It shouldn't be a problem. I won't be in the office for the next two months. I'm starting the data center project, remember?"

"That's right. Okay, that'll make it easier. Well, I guess I'll see you at some point." The car door opened.

"I'll see ya, Jenna," he replied as she scurried from the car.

RYAN CLEARED HIS THROAT. "Jenna, Veronica, thank you for meeting me tonight. I know you've had a long day having just had your first dates, but I wanted to get your first impressions as soon after your date as possible. I'm going to ask you some questions now, okay?"

"Sure," agreed Veronica.

"Yep," Jenna said.

"For starters, Veronica, this wasn't your actual first date with Cameron, but it was your first date with him in five years. How did it feel to be alone with him again after all that time?

Veronica swallowed and wrung her hands as she

replied, "It felt strange and familiar. We have this knowledge of one another—history—and it came up."

"Was it difficult to discuss?"

She nodded, "It was. I didn't totally get over the breakup, or him and now, after all this time, to find myself matched with him... It's like having my biggest fear combine with my best dream."

"What are you afraid of?" Ryan prodded.

"I guess I'm afraid of being rejected, again, or maybe that he was right to leave."

"I'd like to explore that more next time, but for now, one last question: What was the highlight of your date?"

She smiled for the first time. "Everything was amazing—the room, that glorious view—but the icing for me was playing Scrabble. I know it's a normal thing, boring even, but with him it was fun."

"Now Jenna, this was your first date with Parker, but you know him as well, right? You work together," Ryan said, turning toward her.

"We do, and we were hoping that until the last date broadcast you could leave our real names out of the story. And also, no pictures."

Ryan cleared his throat. "I'm not the final say on this, but I'll run it up the chain. Are you concerned about losing your jobs?"

"Um, no, not that. It's just—people talk and sometimes gossip is unkind. Until we know if this could be something, we agreed to wait. Does that make sense?"

"It does. How did that conversation go?"

"Well, actually. I couldn't ignore my concern so I told him how I felt and he was great about it. He totally understood. It was his idea to see if you'd keep our identities hidden until the decision."

Ryan nodded. "So, you found a solution that works for both of you."

"We did."

"What did you like about the date with Parker?"

"It was easier than I had expected. I don't know if it's because we've seen one another at work or if it has something to do with each growing up with a big family, but we had no problem making conversation and he was sweet."

Ryan cocked his head. "Sweet, how?"

"He constantly refilled my glass and fed me chocolate. He also really listened, not like some dates when you can tell they're just waiting to talk," Jenna finished.

"Well, this certainly sounds promising on both fronts. I think I've got enough for today. I'll discuss your request to keep thing anonymous until the last date and let you know what my boss says."

"Thank you, Ryan." Jenna stood and so did Veronica.

"You're welcome," he said as he walked to the door.

"Say hi to Lanie for us."

"Will do. Good night, ladies."

"Good night," they both said at once.

5

LET'S TRY (Two Weeks Later)

"Brr," Ryan shivered as he came inside. He made his way toward the kitchen where Lanie was standing barefoot and stuffing bell peppers. Her sweatshirt dress protruded and her belly touched the island as she worked. "Hello, wife," he said and kissed her neck.

She held out her hands, which were covered with rice and raw meat. "Sorry, I can't touch you."

It didn't stop him from touching her. He leaned close to her mouth and kissed her once sweetly, the second time with demand, and finally his tongue violated her mouth as his hands pinched her breasts. She panted and he turned up the heat by slowly sinking down the length of her body.

Now on his knees, his fingers made a lazy trail along her ankles, calves, and inner thighs. Her throat caught as he raised her dress with excruciating leisure until finally reaching the band of her panties. Gently he pulled each side and with continued sloth, he tugged the sheer white underwear until they were around her ankles.

His hungry mouth acted with none of the reserve he

managed in her undressing as his fiendish tongue plundered her slit, instantly taking her to the edge of orgasm. The pleasure was dizzying. She clutched for the counter and arched forward as he pressed his face to her and clawed at her hips. She ran her food-covered fingers into his hair then tugged, bringing him to stand.

He dove for her mouth kissing her greedily as she released his belt and dropped his pants. He lifted her onto the counter and slid inside of her. Her hands dug into his hair. His palms devastated her breasts. They pulsed in rhythm until they were one, their bond completed by the child between them. Clinging to each other, they screamed united in ecstasy.

"That was quite a welcome," Lanie purred in his ear.

"I guess I missed you today."

She laughed cheekily and tossed her disheveled hair, "I guess you did."

Ryan cleared his throat with a smile and helped her down from the counter.

"The realtor called again today," she said as she watched him pull on his pants. "She left a voice message. There are a few new listings and one that may go on the market. She wants to show us houses again this weekend."

"What do you think? Are we ready to give it another chance?"

Sliding the tray of peppers into the oven, she snickered sarcastically. "I don't think we have a choice. As much as I love it here, a steel and glass river house isn't exactly good for a baby. My place is a little better, but it's tiny and there's no outdoor space. This kicking child," she walked over to Ryan and placed his hand on her belly, "is going to need a room of its own."

"It's moving," he exclaimed while kneeling. "Hey little

one, sorry about all the ruckus before. You'll find out soon enough how demanding your Mommy can be."

She smacked his head and he stood. "Should we make it for Saturday then? I'm interviewing the guys on Sunday after date two."

"Great. I'll email her to confirm. I hope she has some better options this time around," Lanie said.

"The right house will come; we just have to be patient. As much as I'd like to find something soon and get settled before he or she comes, we don't have to. The baby won't need their own room for a while."

"You make so much sense, husband. Now I know why I married you."

"I'm glad it finally came to you."

———

"HAVE YOU SEEN MY BRUSH?" Jenna yelled at the walls.

"What? I can't hear you!" Veronica replied.

Jenna stomped into the living room. "My brush, have you seen it?"

Veronica held the offending brush out for her friend. "Sorry, I didn't know you needed it. It's not as if your hair ever misbehaves."

Jenna snatched it from her hand and vigorously brushed her already smooth hair. "I'm really nervous, V. I don't know if I can go through with this. There's a lot at stake with my job. I'm up for a promotion and I have to ask myself how this decision would look to my boss. My priorities used to be clear and now this matchmaking game has thrown me off course."

Veronica snickered cynically. "I know how hard you've worked. I also know you deserve a man in your life. That boy is fine and I think you might like him, which could be scaring you. Why don't you get through tonight and see how you feel?"

"And if I feel great, if I enjoy myself as I did last time? What then?"

Veronica's dark eyes grew wide and she advanced toward her friend. Reaching up she gripped her shoulders, "Then you fly to outer space where no one on earth will know of your love."

Jenna shook her off. "A lot of help you are."

"Listen, I think you're freaking out because you like him, and maybe you see the potential. That makes total sense. Just don't rule it out. If he's your person, there is a way."

Jenna pivoted to turn things around on her. "Speaking of which, how are you feeling about seeing Cameron again, again?"

Veronica shook her head. "You know, I've been all over the place with this. One minute I'm excited about the match and his wanting to pursue it. It's something I've imagined more times than you know, and you know a lot. On the flip side, I'm still pretty mad and hurt that he abandoned me for Kyra. How do I get over that?"

Jenna's expression was contemplative, "I'm not sure you can. You need a do over, but only you know if that's possible. I'll give you the same advice you gave me. See how you feel after tonight."

Veronica looked worried and the resounding knock at the door meant it was time to *see*.

THE DO IT Yourself bar was a trendy combination of arts, crafts, and spirits. The space was fashioned with sturdy work tables, metal chairs, and industrial-grade lighting.

With shelves filled with tools, and not a child in sight, it was the perfect date experience.

Cameron and Veronica began unpacking their kit as the server arrived with their drinks. "Who has the beer?"

Cameron announced, "That's me, thanks."

She set their drinks down. "Come back to the bar if you want another round."

"Thank you," Veronica said.

Cameron sipped his beer while scanning the combination bar and activity center, "What a cool idea this place is."

"Isn't it? Have you been here before?"

"No, never. This'll be fun. I'm excited to make a map of the United States. With our history and you wielding a hammer, what could go wrong?"

She averted her eyes to focus on the kit and began removing the contents, finding a pouch of nails, a map, tape, two colors of thread, paint, and a wooden base. When everything was laid out, she read the instructions. "This is pretty simple. First, we paint our base black or brown and let it dry. Next, we tape this map to the front of it—and do you see these dots?"

Cameron leaned until they were head to head. "Yes."

"We tap a nail in at every dot. When that's done, we pull off the paper and the fun begins. We add the thread."

He looked at the picture and back at Veronica. "It sounds doable. I'll get the tools and paint. What color do you want?"

"Umm, either works, you pick."

"Okay, I'll be right back."

Veronica sipped her wine as she watched Cameron cross the room. He looked good in his dark denim and thick green sweater. He exuded confidence, which she found to be one of his most appealing qualities. She flashed back on his other attributes and reminded herself that he'd walked away from her once. He could easily do it again. Still, there was no denying their attraction as he returned to the table.

He joked, "Did you miss me?"

She rolled her eyes. "What, over the past five years or just now when you got the hammers?" She opened the paint container and plucked up one of the brushes.

"Ouch. I guess I deserved that."

She slapped the black paint on the wooden base and felt deflated. Veronica knew that her moods over the last few minutes mirrored the range of thoughts she'd entertained since their second-first date—all over the place. Calling him out didn't help. "I'm sorry."

"It's okay. I understand. We were just getting started and I thought things were going well..."

It sounded like the last part of his statement was a question. "But?"

"Kyra and I had unfinished business. Things happened with us that we never really addressed and when she came back around, with the timing of the job in LA, and how you were so casual when I mentioned the opportunity... I guess, I didn't know if you were into me long term."

Her eyes narrowed and her speech was rapid fire. "Wait a minute! Are you putting this on me?"

"No. I'm not at all, but don't you remember? I was ready to move forward. I thought we were great together but I never knew for sure what you were feeling. When I told you I loved you, you didn't say it back."

Veronica sat motionless. Her dark eyes were affixed to the table. How could she tell him today, after their absence, what she was unable to express five years ago? She'd held it long enough—held him responsible. It was time to free them both. She finally rasped, "I was afraid."

"Afraid?" he asked.

She nodded.

"Of what?" He waited as she struggled to find the words.

"Of needing you and you leaving me. Which you did anyway. I thought I'd feel less abandoned if I could convince myself it was mutual." She inhaled sharply and with her exhale came the words that would make her vulnerable. "I never would have left you though. I was crazy about you."

Cameron leaned forward and placed his hands on her wrists, "I didn't know. I'm sorry for what happened, for the lost time. Is it possible for us to start over?"

Veronica contemplated Cameron. Her eyes threatened tears as she replied, "I think we should try."

⸺

JENNA AND PARKER stood at the counter. Their aprons were secured and their attention focused on the stout chef's instructions. "Good evening, everyone. I am Chef Andy and tonight we will be making pan roasted chicken and sautéed vegetables. Let's start by seasoning our chicken. In front of you, you'll find a number of dried and fresh spices available for your use. Begin by selecting the flavors that work for you and your partner. Sprinkle and rub them on your chicken, covering it well.

"When that's done, start dicing the vegetables. You'll find squash, kale, carrots, spinach, and tomatoes. You can even add potatoes, but remember they take longer to cook. Cut the squash and the carrots stew style so they can sit with the sauces without being overcooked. Go ahead and get started. I'll walk around to see how everyone is doing. Don't forget, the wine is bottomless so drink up."

Parker faced Jenna and said, "This is pretty cool."

"Yeah," she agreed. "I love cooking."

"Me too and I'm always looking for new recipes."

Grateful for the task, Jenna asked, "What do you want to season the chicken with?"

"Hmm," he considered the options. "We could go with a simple rosemary, garlic, pepper blend or possibly ginger, cayenne, and lemon…or…"

"Rosemary, garlic, and pepper. I was thinking the same. It'll work with the vegetables too."

"Perfect," he said as they put on plastic gloves. "I'll dice the garlic if you'll strip the rosemary."

Jenna had no difficulty separating her work persona from the date and she found another commonality between them. They had cooking chemistry. Maybe Veronica was on to something. The right relationship was worth more than a job.

Parker's gaze was focused on peeling garlic as he asked, "How have you been over the past couple of weeks?"

"Pretty good. Busy with work, as you know, and getting ready for the holidays. Thankfully, we draw names so I don't have to get presents for everyone in the family. What about you?"

"I've been busy too. We're working ten-hour days on the data center project. Otherwise, I've doing the same, getting ready for Christmas. My family does a Secret Santa thing. We draw names and the person receiving the gift has to guess who gave it to them."

"That's a great idea!"

"Yeah," he said, "we have fun with it. What do you think? Are we ready to season the chicken?"

"Sure," she agreed then drizzled olive oil over the meaty thighs.

Parker smeared garlic on the pieces. "This is like ten cloves. I hope you don't mind." He smiled shyly.

Jenna liked the embarrassment that played across his face and she shared it. "Don't worry, the rosemary and lemon will balance it out."

When all the ingredients were added they set the chicken aside and threw away their gloves. That's when Chef arrived at their station. His beefy hands were clasped across his belly and his dark hair was tousled to the height of fashion "Well, hello, lovebirds. You are that couple from the newspaper, right? They told me you'd be here."

Jenna felt the flush rise to her cheeks and Parker suppressed a grin as he replied, "We are that couple, Chef Andy."

He nodded and peered over the table. "So far looks good. What vegetables will you use?" He looked from Jenna to Parker.

Parker gestured toward Jenna. She shrugged and asked more than stated, "All of them?"

The chef directed his question at Parker. "What do you think?"

"Sounds amazing."

Chef's bushy eyebrows rose as he commanded, "Get your wine," and as an afterthought he added, "please."

Parker and Jenna picked up their glasses.

Chef announced, "Here's to, 'It sounds amazing.' Cheers."

They gingerly tapped glasses and sipped their wine as Chef sauntered away.

"He's formidable," Parker whispered as he started dicing potatoes.

She chuckled softly, "Only if you work for him. Otherwise, he's a teddy bear."

"Do you know him?" Parker asked.

"No, I don't, but I've heard a few things. By the way, are you really good with all the vegetables?"

"Definitely. I was squeamish about tomatoes when I was a kid. Now I eat them every day."

They were quiet for a while, working like a team to create a rainbow of colors from the vegetables and lemons. Orange squash, dark green kale, wheels of yellow citrus, and purple carrots littered their cutting board. Jenna stopped to sip her wine and glanced toward Parker. His attention was on her and the look in his eyes wasn't professional.

She coughed as Chef Andy called everyone to attention. "I'm seeing some good combinations so far. It's time to sear your chicken. We'll be using the cast iron pans. Get them hot with butter, olive oil, and maybe a slice or two of lemon. Medium-high temperature on the burner. When this"—he held up the timer—"goes off, add your chicken and place the lid over the top. Set your timer to four minutes and flip the chicken. Add more butter or oil and cook for another four minutes. I'll be making the rounds."

Parker jumped to attention and fired up the burner. Jenna added half a stick of butter, a healthy pour of olive oil, and several slices of lemon.

Parker tossed in a sprig of rosemary and commented, "It smells good already." He raised his glass and held Jenna's attention. "Here's to cooking chemistry."

Jenna felt like he was reading her mind but she kept her expression neutral. "To cooking."

He chuckled, "Are you okay?"

"Sure," she stammered. "Why wouldn't I be?"

The timer rang and Chef called out. "Time to add the chicken. Set your timers for four minutes."

Parker used tongs and slowly placed the chicken into the oil. The sizzling sound was gratifying but quickly muffled by the lid. "Okay, all set for four minutes," Jenna said as she replaced the timer on the counter.

She sipped her wine and asked, "Maybe it's a taboo subject but we do work together. How is the data center addition going?"

Parker instantly sobered as he replied, "We hit a couple of snags this week with the EC and the low volt guys, but nothing major."

"Typical. What was the problem?"

"Oh, you know, the usual finger pointing. It's worked out now. I removed the communication barrier and with all that transparency, I expect a vast improvement."

"Does that mean you're all up in their shit?"

"It does."

"Nice tactic."

"Why, thank you. What about you? How are your projects doing?"

"Umm, I'm wrapping the Jones School wing addition next week. Really, it's just down to some finish items," she shook her head, "and a backordered fire door. I expect we'll turn it over to the client by the end of next week. The retail store is almost done too, but that was a pretty small project. My biggest challenge now is the new brewery downtown. We're behind schedule and I need to find a pick-up. I finally negotiated a closer staging area with the city. That will help efficiency some."

The buzzer went off. "I'll flip it," Parker said.

Jenna leaned against the counter and watched him in action. His hands were sure as he removed the hot lid with a towel and flipped the chicken expertly. She reset the timer and suggested, "Should we add the potatoes now?"

"You read my mind."

Jenna collected a mound of diced potatoes and added

them to the chicken. Parker gave the pan a shake to settle everything and replaced the lid.

"Nice teamwork, you two. I'd add a dash of white wine," Chef commented as he strolled past.

They exchanged looks and shrugged simultaneously. "He's got a point," Jenna said and uncorked the white wine. Parker opened the lid as she added a splash. Steam rose along with the tantalizing sound of oil and wine warring against iron. For good measure, she added another pour.

Parker purred suggestively, "Mmm, this is going to be so good."

The wine and activity was bringing down her guard. She found herself leaning into the evening, into Parker. They played off of each other in the kitchen as if they had the recipe memorized.

"So," she ventured, "do you have a specialty? A dish you love to make?"

He sipped his wine and smirked. "I'm into pasta. Like homemade noodles, scratch sauces, and I'm experimental. I like to play with my food. What about you?"

"I love Thanksgiving, homemade cranberry and pineapple sauce, sausage and apple stuffing, creamed spinach, and sweet potatoes in raspberry sauce. Oh, and turkey, of course."

"That sounds amazing. Too bad I had to miss it," he paused, "this year." He placed a hand on her hip and she quivered silently.

Buzz. The timer went off.

"Everyone, attention," called Chef. "Now is the time to add the squash then carrots. For those that already started potatoes, stir and leave them at the bottom before adding the other vegetables."

Parker lifted the lid as Jenna layered first the squash

and next the carrots. She sprinkled in a bit of salt for good measure.

"Now," Chef's voice reached through the room, "add two cups of water to the pan and replace the lid. Set the timer for fifteen minutes.

Parker added the water against the protesting heat and replaced the lid.

"Great, everyone. Now let's start dessert. Take the small casserole dish." He held one up for comparison. "You will also find a container with bread, a mixing bowl, eggs, and cream. There are a few special ingredients like brown sugar, vanilla, dark rum, blackberries, semi-sweet chocolate pieces, and butter. Whisk the eggs together with cream and a little rum, a little more if you like. Lay two of the bread slices in the casserole, add chocolate pieces and berries and slices of butter on top, then put the other two slices of bread above, like a sandwich. Add more butter, berries, sugar, and chocolates. When that's done, slowly pour the egg mixture into the casserole and place it into the preheated oven beneath you. Set that timer for 45 minutes. Once again, I'll be circling the stations."

Parker and Jenna quickly located the ingredients. Jenna whisked the eggs while Parker added cream, rum, plus a dash of vanilla. She finished it off with a scoop of sugar and stirred while he placed the first two slices of bread in the dish. Their fingers grazed as they dispersed generous mounds of berries and chocolate onto the bread. Adding the second layer, they repeated the process. "Now for the magic," Jenna's light eyes shone with excitement. "Rum mix."

Parker joked, "It was more of a pour than a dash."

Jenna laughed, "Yes, it was." With their dessert settled in the oven, she took another sip of her endless glass of wine. "I'm glad we're not driving tonight."

"That's for sure. I like the feeling though. After the past two weeks, this is just the kind of night I need." He leaned forward and his eyes gravitated toward her mouth.

Buzz. The timer drenched them with reality.

"All right, everyone. Let's check the chicken. Now is the time to add your greens and a small amount of water if called for."

Parker backed away and used the towel to remove the lid. The stock was cooked down to a light brown jus. Jenna said, "I'll add the kale and spinach and more water."

He waited as she included the items and another splash of white wine. "I'm starving now,"

Parker complained and Jenna got a glimpse of the irresistible boy he must have been. His golden hair looked so soft, she had to stop herself from touching it. "You'll live. Let's set the timer for five minutes."

"Okay, chefs. You've done your part; now is the time for you to sit. Please follow the hostess to the next room and bring your wine glasses. We'll serve dinner shortly."

They entered a sparsely furnished dining room with floor to ceiling windows and tables covered in white paper. Upon each, a solitary candle flickered softly and a red rose in a narrow glass bottle lent a romantic touch. Outside, passersby moved quickly against the chilly December wind.

The moment they sat, a waiter came around to refill their wine. Parker smiled happily as he thanked him and turned his attention back to Jenna. "I'm excited to see how our dinner turns out."

"Me too," she agreed.

He looked intently at her. "If we were at work, I couldn't say this, but since we aren't, I'm just going to tell you. You look beautiful."

She met his attentive stare with more confidence than

she felt. "So do you. I mean, not beautiful, but…you know what I mean."

He chuckled, "Thank you. It took me hours to do my hair."

She mocked, "I can only imagine."

"In all seriousness, I know this isn't simple, but I'm happy to be here with you. The last couple of weeks have given me time to think about the future and the kind of life I hope to build. I don't want to scare you, but I could see you in it, Jenna."

His words took her breath away. She hadn't allowed herself to think too far down that path. Even when her restless mind inevitably trailed to him and their day at the winery, she talked herself back to reality, placing him and the Love Test aside. Tonight, sitting across from him, his spicy cologne lingering between them, she found herself falling. Still, she wasn't ready to bare herself and fortunately she didn't have time to reply, as their dinner arrived.

"Good evening again," said Chef Andy as he set their beautifully presented dinner plates before them. "I was impressed at the ease you found in the kitchen and I couldn't help but test your dish. You did a splendid job. Bon appétit."

"Thank you, Chef," they chimed.

Left with nothing but the air between them and the tantalizing aroma of their culinary creation, they shared a meal they would never forget.

———

VERONICA AND CAMERON RODE home in silence. The steam they'd let out talking about the past and working to finish the map project was building again as they neared her house. They pulled to a stop and Cameron insisted, "I'll walk you to the door."

Veronica felt conflicted between nerves and comfort. She knew Cameron. She'd once loved him, but was he the same person? Was she? Her thoughts were clouded by fear as they arrived on her porch. Cameron set the map on the ground and placed his hands on her shoulders. For a moment they stared, motionless, expectant. The only thing breaking the silence was the jingle of the keys in her hand.

He stooped down and leaned in for a kiss. Her heart was pounding now and the nervousness all but over-whelmed her until his soft, familiar lips grazed hers. Her missing Cameron was back. His knowing tongue helped her forget the past, if only for a time. The softest memo-ries, his gentle hands, the way their bodies used to fit, it all flooded her and she found herself wanting it to be real. He pulled back and rested his forehead against hers. "Thank you for tonight, Veronica, and for giving us another chance. I won't mess up again."

The words she'd been longing to hear flooded her with hope and nearly brought her to tears. She couldn't allow that so she pushed her emotions down with a quip: "You'd better not." With that she slid the key into the lock and ducked inside.

"Wait a minute," Cameron called.

"Yes?"

"The map," he said while handing it to her.

"No," she said. "You keep it. It'll help you remember not to mess up."

He smiled softly and replied, "I don't need a reminder, V. Until our next date…"

JENNA AND PARKER held hands on the ride home. His fingers caressed her palms and wrist, sending shivers along her back. The concern over their work situation took a backseat to the connection they were building. Though she expected to tell him about the promotion she'd applied for, she couldn't bring herself to ruin the evening with work. The night didn't clarify the situation, but for the time being, she was happy to be in the moment with him.

They arrived at her house and he automatically got out of the car to walk her to the door. When they stopped at the porch, he pulled her near. With their bodies so close, it was impossible to know which of them was moving. Perhaps, it was a gravitational force that slowly drew them together. When their lips finally met, the world went quiet. Jenna stopped thinking and melted into the kiss. His tongue was unhurried and she met his pace. It was the sweetest torture. When they pulled apart, they were panting.

Parker whispered, "I know we have things to talk about, but for right now, I want you to know tonight was special to me. Thank you."

Jenna didn't leave him hanging as she agreed, "Thank you, Parker. Tonight was special to me too."

"I can't wait until our next date, Jenna."

She liked the way he said her name and the softness he brought out in her. She kissed him once more, on the cheek. "Until then, Parker."

THE NEIGHBORHOOD COFFEE shop was bustling with activity as the Sunday morning crowd enjoyed their specialty brews and breakfast bites. A toddler tossed a spoon onto the concrete floor and the frother exploded with hot air as beverages were made. Ryan ordered a coffee and headed for a table in the corner.

Moments later, Cameron arrived and after getting a cup of his own, he joined Ryan. The men shook hands and sat. Ryan asked, "How are you today?"

"Great," Cameron beamed.

"Does that mean the dates are going well?"

Cameron's expression was hopeful as he replied, "I think it does."

"What did you guys do last night?"

"We went to this DIY bar and made a map of the Unites States out of nails and thread."

Ryan chuckled, "How'd it turn out?"

Cameron replied, "I was hesitant at first, but with Veronica's mind for instructions, it worked out."

The sparkle in his eye was impossible to miss. Ryan never considered himself a romantic man. In fact, most of his life was devoted to the harsher side of humanity, but his restless desire to shed light on tragedy was less now that he had Lanie in his life. He wondered if Cameron found the same serenity with Veronica. "You two have a past."

Cameron nodded, "We do."

"I assume you've had some conversation about what happened."

"Yes, we have."

"And?" His one-word question was anything but simple.

"You know, it took us five years to admit what we were feeling back then and why things happened the way they did."

"Why did you leave her?"

Cameron stared into his coffee cup. "Honestly, I was floundering with my career and insecure in general. At the time, it seemed like she wasn't sure about the relationship and I let a girlfriend from my past get in my head. When a job in California coincided with my ex wanting to reconcile, I made the wrong choice."

Ryan felt badly putting the guy against the ropes, but he had a job to do, so he pressed. "Why did you think that Veronica was unsure?"

He inhaled deeply then blurted, "Because I'm an idiot."

"Well," Ryan chuckled, "the first step is acknowledging the problem."

Cameron laughed.

"In all seriousness," Ryan continued, "there must have been a reason."

"I want to tell you, but I don't want her hurt or embarrassed by what I share."

Ryan was no stranger to the delicate dance required of him as a journalist, particularly in this situation where matters of the heart were at play. "I can't say she won't be embarrassed by what you share, but you have my commitment that I will weigh my words carefully as I write the article."

Cameron's hands circled the mug as he admitted, "When I told her that I loved her, she didn't say it back. I wasn't thinking about anything except my hurt ego. I thought it was about me, that she wasn't in love with me."

"What do you think now?"

"It's not what I think. It's what I know."

"And?"

"Veronica's parents were drug addicts so she was raised by her aunt. I didn't understand how hard it was for her to be vulnerable or what it meant for her to love. She was afraid to count on me and who could blame her after her start?"

Ryan felt a pang of empathy for Veronica. Not only

had she been abandoned by the people who were genetically wired to care for her, but Cameron had done the same. "Do you think you guys can overcome this?"

Cameron's expression was earnest as he replied, "Last night we agreed to try. We realized how much we both messed up, me especially. I hope I can make it up to her."

This brought Ryan to the questions he'd planned. "If it weren't for the algorithm matching you, would you have contacted her again?"

"I wanted to, but I doubt I would have because I didn't think there was a chance."

"Does this mean you're going to see the challenge through?"

"Definitely."

———

PARKER DUCKED through the doorway as he made a beeline for Ryan. They shook hands.

"Nice to see you again, Parker."

"You too, Ryan. Though I have to admit, I'm a little nervous."

Ryan studied Parker and asked, "What are you uneasy about?"

"Everything, really. I work with Jenna and I'm starting to like her, a lot. I've never been interviewed before and I don't want to say anything dumb."

Ryan found it funny that the strong construction foreman was nervous, but he did his best to put him at ease. "You don't need to worry. I'm not writing an exposé."

Parker nodded. "I guess that's true."

"Listen, I understand your work situation and I agree with keeping things anonymous."

"Thanks," Parker said.

"Do you think that knowing each other as work colleagues has helped or hindered the dating process?"

The corners of Parker's mouth raised slightly as he replied. "Both. Some things, like talking to her, are easy because we already know each other."

"What else?"

"I wondered if we'd spend all of our time talking about work and that hasn't been the case. We have a lot of commonalities outside of construction, but we both love our jobs."

Ryan didn't miss the shadow that crossed his face as he said the last part. "Are you concerned the work situation will become an issue?"

"I'm trying not to be but there is reality. I wouldn't want to do anything to make her uncomfortable and I'm not excited about people finding out."

This perked Ryan's attention. "Why not?"

"We work in construction. Jenna is the only female project manager in the company. She's already the topic of a lot of whispers. If this comes out, I don't know how we'll handle it. She doesn't want to risk her job or reputation and I don't want to see that happen either."

Parker's worry weighed heavy between them. Ryan knew how locker-room talk went and he could imagine how he'd feel if the situation were reversed. He also didn't miss the fact that Parker's reputation wasn't at risk because of their workplace romance. "If it weren't for the algorithm, would you have asked her out?"

Parker shook his head, "No. I wanted to, but I wouldn't have done it for those reasons. I know how driven she is. It's one of the traits I admire in her. Even if I had asked her out, I don't think she would have agreed because of work."

Ryan could see that Parker was struggling, but he had to ask. "Are you going to see the challenge through?"

Parker contemplated the table for a time and when his eyes finally met Ryan's, he said, "Jenna is one of a kind and this sounds soppy, but I feel like we matched for good reason. I don't know how it will end up, but I need to find out."

6

LET'S BEND

Jenna yelled to Veronica, "Did you pack the curling iron?"

"Got it," she replied from her bedroom.

Jenna entered Veronica's room, carrying two Cosmos. "Look what I have."

Veronica was flushed as she tossed her duffle bag down. "You read my mind."

"That's because, after eleven years of friendship, we share the same one," Jenna smiled.

"Does that mean you're freaking out as much as I am right now?"

"Why do you think I made the cocktails?" Jenna chided.

"How are you feeling about seeing Parker this weekend?"

"Like vomit is boiling in my belly. I'm nervous and…"

Veronica remained silent as Jenna finished her thought.

"I can't believe I'm saying this, also excited. It's a bad decision to stay on this path. It will cause issues at work, but I've been thinking about him a lot since our last date."

Veronica was bursting to know, "And? What do you think about him?"

"He's great. I wish we didn't know each other from work."

Veronica's nod was almost imperceptible. She knew her friend well and the work situation was a big obstacle for her. Jenna had a lot to prove to the world and herself. Finding a man to complement her drive was never going to be easy. She replied, "Maybe the career connection is a good thing. You're a workaholic and Parker is in your field. If he knows that side of you and you have other common- alities, he might be your perfect match."

Jenna cleared her throat as if to signal a subject changed then asked, "What about Cameron? I'm sorry we haven't talked about it much over the past couple of weeks. I wanted to leave you space to work it out. Do you feel ready for this weekend and what comes next?"

A light swept across Veronica's face as the corners of her mouth lifted. "I think so. I've been afraid to say it out loud, not wanting to jinx it, but we had an honest talk about what happened five years ago. I realized I made some mistakes and so did he. We agreed to put the past behind us and I'm...hopeful."

A knock at the door signified the arrival of the men and their awaiting destiny.

———

AS AWKWARD as any double date in high school was, this entourage of adults took jumpy to the max as they ambled along the dark and icy roads in the back of the Cadillac limousine.

"Oh look, champagne," Parker exclaimed. "I'll open it." He pulled off the foil and quickly twisted the cork, only he lost control of it and it flew directly at Jenna's forehead. He leaned forward to check on her as the bubbles from the bottle gushed all over Veronica's pants, causing her to kick her feet into Cameron's shins. Parker quickly righted the bottle in time to watch the results of the mayhem his ineptitude of managing the cork had caused.

Jenna's forehead shone pink at the spot where the cork landed. Cameron was rubbing his legs with a pained look on his face and Veronica was glaring at Parker. To add insult to their injury, in the most inappropriate outburst, he started laughing hysterically. Jenna quickly joined, followed by Cameron and the reluctant Veronica. Parker's fumble created a tension-breaking distraction that forced everyone's guard down.

"That was the least smooth move I've ever seen, buddy," Cameron chuckled.

"Yes, lame!" Veronica shoved Parker.

Jenna held her empty champagne flute to her forehead and feigned agony, "I'm already getting a headache."

Wiping the tears from his eyes was pointless, as another round streamed down. "I'm so sorry, guys. Especially Jenna. Are you okay?" He leaned forward and touched her knee.

She removed the glass from her head and whined, "I will be when you pour the bubbles. That is if there is any left in the bottle."

Parker raised the half full bottle and announced, "A half a glass apiece since Veronica already hogged the rest."

This got Parker another shove and a smack for good measure. "Okay, I deserved that."

He filled Jenna's glass, Veronica's, then Cameron's, who flinched as he approached, causing them another round of giggles, and finally his own. "Here's to breaking the ice."

"Cheers," they chimed.

The rest of the drive to Bend was like a group of old friends getting together. Once they got over their initial weirdness, they found a groove and easy conversation between them. After a time, they pulled off the highway and steered to the right, driving several miles they wound through streets of well-lit and manicured homes and park-sized yards with majestic oaks and soaring evergreens. Covered in the hazy night sky, the moon filtered through the low cloud cover, casting a muted backdrop of grey to black against the blanket of white snow that covered the ground.

"Look, it's snowing," Jenna exclaimed.

"Yes!" Parker added.

They pulled into a recently shoveled driveway of beige stamped concrete and nosed down the circular driveway toward a modern home of glass and steel. The front door blended in with the walkway, and walls of glass gave an unobstructed view through the living room to the stilted balcony past the living room. It was as if the home were floating in the middle of the forest.

"Oh my," Veronica exclaimed with her nose pressed up against the glass.

Suddenly, the door opened and their driver, Troy, saved her from a face-plant by stopping her fall. As red as a beet, she righted herself and stepped from the car. They walked toward the door and waited as the driver entered a code to open it.

"Please go ahead. I'll be back with the bags."

They filed in, Veronica leading the charge, and it was as if they'd landed on the cover of Dwell magazine. Beige concrete floors and furniture in matching hues glowed against the roaring fire and ideal lighting scheme. In the corner stood a woodsy looking Christmas tree with a spray of colorful lights and handmade ornaments upon it. A red skirt pooled at its base and was the only splash of color in the room. Accents of rose gold and white were tastefully distributed and the faux white fur rug added that sexy extra touch to the space. The modern kitchen was snugged into the corner. It boasted a huge island and four velvet chairs.

"Nice digs," Cameron's brows rose as he strode across the living room toward the sliding wall of doors. He pushed one open and a gust of cold air billowed inside. That didn't stop them from following him out.

The deck was bigger than the house and surrounded by a glass half-wall with only a narrow rail at the top. In the darkness of the murky night sky, walking to the end of it felt like walking a plank. They did it anyway. Like expectant children, they lined up at the edge and looked out into the blackest forest, half expecting to see eyes peering back at them. It was silent except for the sound of water dribbling somewhere in the distance.

Veronica's question was nearly a whisper, "I wonder what it will look like in the morning."

Troy's broad frame filled the doorway as he called, "That's it for me for tonight, guys."

They turned to walk toward him. "I'm staying on property. There's a guesthouse down the way. Text me when you want to leave tomorrow. I left my number on the counter."

"Thank you, Troy," Parker said.

"Yes, thanks," Cameron added.

"Good night, Troy," said Jenna.

"Good night," he called.

And Veronica replied almost curtly, "Night."

As he closed the front door, Cameron stood by the fire and asked, "What should we do now?"

The girls looked at one another and Jenna walked toward the hallway, "We're going to check out our bedroom."

They walked the L-shaped hallway and peered inside the first room. There were two beds inside and a wall of glass with a door that led onto the patio, leaving no visual barrier between them and the outdoors. Jenna noticed her and Veronica's bags were left inside. "This is us." She tapped V on the shoulder.

"Great! I get the bed by the window." Veronica cried.

"Why? You won't wake up until after seven. I'll have already finished my first pot of coffee by then," Jenna jabbed.

"Still," she pouted, "I want the outdoors to be the first thing I see in the morning."

"It's yours, princess." Jenna shook her head and left the room. "I want to see the boys' room."

She followed the hallway to a door straight ahead. Another two-person bedroom, only this one had a partition down the center and on each side was that transparency of glass against the unseen wild. King-sized beds in charcoal shrouds faced the dark night and unknown morning that would come soon enough. Parker and Cameron's duffels were left inside the doorway.

"Swanky," Parker said.

"Yeah," Cameron replied. "Which one to you want?"

"Me, um, how about the right?"

"I wanted left so we're good." Turning toward the ladies, he asked, "So what's next?"

"Next?" Jenna asked while looked toward her best friend.

Veronica smiled. "I'm thinking a cup of hot cocoa and bed is in order."

Cameron smirked, "I'll join you."

She shook her head and hissed, "For cocoa."

They found their way into the kitchen and watched as Veronica rooted around in the cupboards finding cocoa powder, cinnamon, and sugar. She headed to the refrigerator and pulled out the milk and found a pan and whisk. Adding the ingredients together, she kicked on the flame and slowly stirred until the cocoa was distributed.

Cameron found mugs and a bottle of brandy and set them on the counter beside her. She shrugged, "Can't hurt, right?"

He smiled and added a healthy pour to each of the cups.

Once the milk had simmered long enough to meet Veronica's discerning taste, she added the nubuck liquid to the mugs. With a final flourish, she dropped a cinnamon stick into each.

"Mmm, cocoa magic," Jenna's eyes sparkled.

They each took one and Jenna said, "Here's to V's delicious hot chocolate and our getting to stay in this unbelievable house. Oh my god, you guys!"

The heat from the milk and spicy brandy warmed them to their toes and put a dreamy filter on the start of their weekend together in Bend.

"And let's hope," Veronica tilted her chin in Parker's direction, "he doesn't spill this." She raised her glass as Cameron nearly choked cocoa.

———

PARKER, Jenna, and Cameron stood at the edge of the deck, seeming to float in the heavy white fog that blanketed the forest behind the house. Evergreens were thinner against the freezing temperatures while oaks and maples stood as outlines in the half-finished canvas of winter. A golden eagle circled above, scanning the terrain for opportunity. Its dark outline and formidable wingspan was dusted with tawny swipes.

"It's peaceful here." Jenna studied the bird with one eye closed. Her blonde hair was pulled into a bun and her thick winter jacket covered her nightshirt.

Parker looked down at Jenna and Cameron knew it was the perfect moment for a kiss so he found his escape. "Think I'll bring V a cup of coffee in bed."

Jenna cleared her throat.

"Not coffee," Cameron met Jenna's gaze, "half warmed milk and half coffee."

She smiled, "Good job and good luck."

Cameron left them and Parker moved closer to Jenna until their hips touched. "I could get used to this," he rasped.

Jenna looked up as he unexpectedly took her face in his hands. He caressed her cheek with his thumb, then kissed her sweetly. For that off-guard moment, she was just a woman, on a date and kissing an attractive man who happened to have the cutest morning hair and looked even hotter with a dusting of stubble.

———

"GOOD MORNING."

Cameron's voice called from the doorway and Veronica fake struggled to wake up. She'd already been up and brushed her teeth and hair. She had jumped back into bed from her window vantage point when she saw Cameron leave Parker and Jenna, but not before she saw them kiss. It was only seven in the morning and already the day looked promising.

She yawned and tousled her hair as she rolled his direction, "Morning."

"I brought your favorite, café au lait."

She purred, "Thank you, sweet man."

"Ha," he half laughed, half coughed, as he noticed the straps on her nightie were quite thin.

She sat against the pillows, adjusted the covers, and accepted the drink. "This is amazing."

His eyes penetrated hers then traveled to her faintly glossed lips as she sipped the coffee. He noticed and appreciated her efforts. "Amazing is the right word for it."

She patted the spot beside her, "Want to sit next to me, check out my view?"

"It's not bad from this vantage point, but I won't say no to that."

He moved to beside her and those vaguely familiar sensations came back to Veronica. His scent was the same, but though she once knew him, he was a foreigner now. The dark hairs that danced along his arms were always there, but she'd forgotten. His sure mouth and clear eyes pinned her once more as they had in the past. Her heart raced as he moved closer.

"Ahh, sorry." Jenna burst into the room with Cameron in tow. "There's a trail practically outside the door. We're thinking about going snowshoeing before breakfast. Any interest?"

Veronica did not want to go snowshoeing before breakfast, but she knew being alone in the house with Cameron was a bad idea. He was looking too intently at her and she could only resist so much. Although she wanted to rip his clothes off, it was too soon to put that much on the line. "I'm in. Give me a few minutes to get ready."

Jenna laughed. "Okay, guys, we'll see you in an hour, maybe two if we're on V time."

"Stop that. I promise to be quick. Now out. Go away, boys. We've got work to do."

The men left them and Veronica practically pounced on Jenna. "I saw you kissing Parker."

Jenna smiled and sat at the end of the bed. "Voyeur."

She replied unabashed, "You know it."

She jabbed, "As if you and Cameron weren't making out."

"Until you threw ice on the situation."

"Sorry."

"No, don't be. I kind of like the suspense of this. Should we talk logistics for later? Do you plan to hook up with Parker?"

"V, you are too much. Do you plan on hooking up with Cameron? Never mind! Don't answer that. Let's get ready and worry about hooking up if the time comes."

She cackled, "That means you haven't ruled it out." Veronica shook her index finger tauntingly toward her friend, "Naughty Jenna is having a workplace romance."

She replied snidely, "Shut up or I'll sit on you."

———

"I'M CERTAIN THIS IS A RECORD," Jenna said as she floated into the living room. Veronica closely followed. "In under an hour, we are ready to leave the house."

"Ha, ha." Veronica rolled her eyes. "You made use of the time."

Parker stood and walked toward Jenna. "It was well worth the wait. You look beautiful."

Jenna had pulled on a cream-colored cap and wore a similar shade turtleneck and dark pants and was carrying her snow boots. Her lips were brick red and her lashes ink black. From Parker's standpoint, she looked like she was ready for a photo shoot.

Veronica stood with her hand upon her hip. Her black pants and thermal shirt were skin tight and her boots matched the stark ensemble. Her lips shone candy apple red and her raven hair dangled from a high pony tail to her shoulder blades.

Cameron hesitated forward, a look of awe made his expression. "I'm going snowshoeing with a supermodel slash superhero."

Veronica pinned him with her sooted lashes and snapped, "Shut it."

"Shall we?" Parker asked.

"Let's go," Jenna said and they made their way toward the front porch, taking a minute to put on their boots and coats. When they were ready, Jenna pointed, "The trail is this way."

The couples set out, walking around the house and to the well-managed trail that was contiguous to the property. The snow and thin layer of ice crunched neatly under their feet and the path was smooth as if they were the first to travel it today. Parker and Jenna walked ahead. Their chemistry was so natural, it seemed they quite knew one another. Veronica and Cameron were silent as they moved under the white sky. The occasional bird called or fluttered off its perch in the trees, startled by their presence. The sound of dripping water grew more pronounced as they followed the road.

Cameron held both poles with his left hand and slid his arm around Veronica's shoulders. She tolerated it briefly, because it was a bold move and she liked that, but she was the smallest of the group and it was hard enough for her to keep up with their long-legged struts without the added weight of his arm to contend with.

He whispered, "Want to find a path of our own?"

His words comingled with a stiff breeze and her nipples instantly responded affirmatively. "No, thank you," she lied. "I'm going with safety in numbers. Whenever they go off trail in the movies, that's when they get whacked."

Cameron hissed as he drew her near, almost tripping her up, "I promise not to whack you."

She shoved him and fell herself with the action. While she was down, she took a moment to smash together a solid snow ball. From hands and knees, she pelted Cameron on the neck. He sputtered as she swiftly crushed another handful of icy snow into a ball. *Whack*, this time it hit him on the forehead. With the third throw, she nailed him in the groin. Instead of cowering, he came for her and lifted her right off the ground, tossing her over his shoulder. He stomped off trail toward a section of trees and called over his shoulder, "See you guys later."

Jenna and Parker looked at one another and shrugged. "Be careful," Jenna yelled.

"From the looks of it, they'll be fine," Parker soothed.

"Yes, I know. Still, I worry about her."

Parker knew how close Jenna and Veronica were and he was aware of the history between Veronica and Cameron. His sense was that he was into her. Was Cameron in love? How would he know? But, he wasn't there against his will. That much was clear. "He seems sincere."

Jenna nodded. "He does. He always did."

"Maybe the timing is better now."

The mention of timing had Jenna traveling down her own rabbit hole of doubt, reminding her exactly how she and Parker became acquainted and what damage it could do to her career. She mumbled, "Timing is everything."

As she said it, a branch snapped ahead. Their eyes

traveled toward the sound and a mature buck stood in the vicinity. He turned to meet their stare, showing them the whites in his eyes. In a gust of powder, he scampered away as if his life depended on it. Let's face it, last month during hunting season, it did.

"He was a nice one," Parker admired as the deer rushed for cover. "Do you want to talk about it, Jenna?"

His straightforward redirect was admirable and also disconcerting. Jenna liked tackling problems head-on at work, but in this situation, with her building interest in him, she was procrastinating. The reason was obvious: Once they got to the end, if the best outcome happened and they wanted to be together, she'd have to decide between her career and him. How could she give up either without having resentments? "Do we have to?"

"Not at the moment, but eventually we do. I like you."

Her heart fluttered at his simple admission. He had laid himself bare and she wanted to give him the same. She stopped moving and held his wrist. "I like you too."

Their kiss lingered in the clarity of mutual desire. His tongue demanded softly and hers played along. Her body vibrated as his hands encircled her waist. Her arms reached for his shoulders, pulling him in. Their snowshoes got the best of them as they tried to get closer. Jenna pulled away and huffed, "Want to go back to the house?"

He guffawed nervously in response. "Yes."

Almost as fast as the buck they'd startled earlier, the two co-workers scampered back toward their home away from home. What took only minutes felt an eternity against the anticipation of what their return would mean. If either of them had reservations, their pace denied time for consideration. Once on the porch, they tugged off their boots and coats and fumbled inside.

Parker turned to Jenna, his fingers wove into her long

blonde hair and her ski cap landed on the ground. His mouth took hers without a second thought. She moaned in response and tugged his sweater over his head. His broad shoulders and confident grin drove her wild.

He followed her lead and teased her sweater overhead. His thumbs edged the sexy pink bra she wore and Jenna panted. Like powerful magnets they clung together, kissing and fondling their way into the first bedroom. Parker cupped Jenna's ass and picked her up to straddle him then tossed her on the bed.

"The door," she breathed, "lock it."

Without a wasted second, he turned the lock and dove onto the bed. They laid inches apart. He rested on his elbow, eyes fastened to hers and something electric transpired between them. With his free hand, he brushed a strand of hair from her cheek. Making a trail with his finger, he followed it down her throat, over her collarbone and down her sternum. His lazy fingers rested there for a moment before continuing their light trail toward her stomach. He rasped, "Are you okay with this?"

Jenna had no words; only her suffocating desire for Parker existed. She nodded yes and let the consequences fall away.

His hands hooked the sides of her pants and panties and he smoothly moved down the length of her body, tossing them to the floor. Before she could blink, he'd returned to her side and with one hand under her back, snapped her bra to open. Those gentle hands wasted no time in adding her last article of clothing to the floor. Parker's eyes met hers and his smile grew childlike. He scanned her body and faced her again, "You are in so much trouble."

Jenna didn't realize she'd been holding her breath waiting for his reaction. She was naked in front of Parker and she was happy. His mouth took hers as she fumbled with his belt and the buttons of his jeans. He pulled back and kissed her throat, trailing his tongue down her center and stopping to mouth one of her tiny pink nipples. She groaned and slid her hand into his pants as he jerked forward. The friction of his tongue and her stroke was intense and they needed more. She tugged Parker's pants down. He stood and dropped them to the floor as she stole a peek at his perfection.

He lunged back onto the bed and hovered over Jenna. Her legs wrapped around his waist as he found his way inside her world. She squeaked seductively and it drove him mad. His hands teased her breasts and his thumbs pressed against her diamond nipples. Her fingers raked through his hair and along his spine. As he moved deeper inside of her, she met him with every stroke. Their mouths glued and tongues danced as if they'd been acquainted for a hundred years. Whatever caution they once felt was gone. His throat caught, "Come for me, Jenna. I want to make you come."

She knew what he wanted because she wanted it too. "Together. Let's come together." She squealed as he bit her nipple and thrust himself deeply. She tightened around him, holding him in place until they couldn't wait another second. Their mutual orgasm rang throughout the house as they fused in rapture.

___

THE BLOOD WAS RUSHING to her head and her belly ached at the spot where his shoulder held her. "Would you put me down now?"

He gritted, "Just a minute." Stubbornly, he dug in and walked up a hill.

The sound of water grew louder as they arrived at the base of an enormous evergreen. In view was a rock wall with a trickling waterfall. Cameron set Veronica on her feet against the tree. It was slightly warmer under its shelter and the wind wasn't whipping.

She was at once miffed and awed. "Guess the best stuff really is off trail."

Cameron trained in on her like a laser. His brown eyes held hers. His emotions were volatile beneath the rigid surface. The strain was evident. He wasn't tasteful about it as he destroyed her lipstick with his possessive mouth.

His hands went places he'd only dreamed of visiting again as he glided over her sweater, teasing her yearning breasts with his torturous skims. She huffed and he pressed himself against her, her back firmly held by the tree. "I want you, V. Now."

She couldn't talk; the throbbing was ringing in her ears. He tugged her waistband and kneeled at her feet, burying his tongue and demanding to play. She shuddered from the shock of it—his mouth, the setting. What was happening? Her body betrayed her as she whimpered under his command.

She tugged his hair. He stood and faced her. Their dark eyes locked. Cameron pecked Veronica's full lips. Her scent lingered between them. His tongue delved inside, tapping voltage into her desire.

"Turn around."

Veronica wanted to obey him. She liked the fact that he was telling her what to do, for now anyway. She faced the tree as he dropped his pants. With one hand he cupped her generous breast and with the other, his fingers glided inside of her. "Lean forward," he hissed.

Veronica throbbed with anticipation as she arched her back and gave him what he wanted. He entered and it all came rushing back: their weekends together, the late-night cooking sessions, the way their bodies fit. How could they have let it go? The time apart didn't diminish their knowledge of one another. The places only he could reach with his bittersweet nuzzle had merely hibernated. That soft opening he had once refused was again within his grasp.

The bark was cold and a grounding reminder against his decadent teasing. He tortured her breasts and clitoris with knowing strokes. His tongue and teeth joined in the merriment as he nibbled the crook of her neck. He filled her and she accepted all of him. Air was visible as she huffed at his every stroke. His hands trailed her spine and stopped at her hips. His thumbs scandalously massaged her tail bone and she gasped.

Cameron pulled her to almost standing and holding her breast he glided like molasses. Knowing it was what he wanted, she gave him control and the pleasure of it was extreme. Though his moves were kind, she felt his power. She submitted to his hands, to him and it wouldn't stop there. His finger teased forbidden spots and her body betrayed her with wetness.

"I remember," he whispered almost menacingly.

The torture moved to her breasts, pinching until she whimpered. "Have you had enough?" he demanded.

"Yes."

"What was that?" He pumped a little faster.

"I want to come."

His hand circled her neck, "Say it again, V."

"I want to come." She whimpered, "You're going to make me come."

His thrusts lost leisure. He moved as if climbing a set of spiral stairs, racing to see the view of a lifetime and she was running with him. Her ass bounced from his sensual battering. The primal song of their bliss exploded into the outdoors, setting a flock of birds to flight and echoing in the stark morning light.

PARKER'S WEIGHT grounded Jenna in reality as she struggled to comprehend what had just happened. Going into the weekend, she made a pact with herself not to let things go this far with him. That was an easier story to tell when he wasn't near. Something about Parker—no, everything about Parker—was inviting.

He raised his head, making eye contact. "Am I smashing you?"

She shook her head, "No."

His eyes danced in the glow of the morning light and his mouth pulled into a soft smile. "That was unexpected."

She exhaled. "Yes, it was."

His lips sought hers and as gently as a breeze, he coaxed her mind blank. His sweet tongue told love stories his lips could not yet form. He'd thought of her like this for the better part of a year. The added six weeks of torturously slow courtship overwhelmed his senses and drove him to finally actualize his thoughts. The experience of Jenna far outshined his imagination. She was softer than he'd expected, shy and so pliant. Even now as they kissed, her willingness was a shudder to his soul. They were more than a possibility. They were real.

The front door opened and Veronica called out, "Jenna, Parker, are you here?"

Jenna wriggled under Parker's weight. Her eyes grew wide as she pushed him off of her. "Oh my god. They're here."

The two scrambled around the room, finding and putting on clothes. Jenna's sweater was on and she struggled to pull up the snug pants. Parker jumped into his jeans and sweater as Jenna whisper-yelled, "Hurry, let's go out on the deck."

Parker scrambled behind her as she tiptoed across the room. "The lock," he remembered. He jumped to the door to slide the lock as Jenna opened the slider to the frigid outdoors. They sat at a small table outside as Veronica and Cameron found them. "There you are," Veronica demanded.

"Here we are," Parker confirmed.

If Veronica's arched brow were any indication, she noticed his disheveled hair and Jenna's tangled mane. "What have you kids been up to?" she sneered.

"Just enjoying the scenery," Parker covered.

Cameron spoke up, "We were thinking of having breakfast then getting into town for the day. Any takers?"

Jenna spoke up, "Sure. I'll make a frittata and we can head out afterward."

"Yum," Cameron said.

"Great," Jenna replied nervously, "I'd better get started."

Veronica solicited, "Do you need any help."

Jenna's expression was droll as she responded, "As if you would be helpful in the kitchen. Nope, I've got it."

Parker rose to his feet and said, "I'll give you a hand."

Veronica spoke up, "I'll make the mimosas!"

Cameron got on board, "I'll assist."

As naturally as their second date, Parker and Jenna found an easy yin and yang in the kitchen. She diced potatoes and bacon as he whipped the eggs and sliced cheese. The aroma wafted throughout the house, tickling Veronica and Cameron's noses all the way on the deck.

"Smells amazing," Cameron yelled toward the house.

"It'll be ready in ten," Jenna replied as Parker joined them on the deck with the champagne bottle in hand.

"Refill?" he asked Veronica.

"Yes, please."

"You?" He directed his question to Cameron.

"We aren't driving. Fill me up."

"So, Parker…" Veronica's tone raised the hairs on his neck.

"Yes, Veronica?" he replied.

"Take a seat. I'd like to get to know you better."

He found his way into the smallish wrought iron chair and asked, "What do you want to know?"

"I have just one question."

He swallowed.

"What are your intentions with Jenna?"

He choked in response and Veronica kept it coming. "That's not the reaction I was hoping for."

He chuckled, "Well, I didn't expect you to go all dad with a shotgun on me."

Cameron laughed. "Obviously, you don't know V."

She kicked his already sore shin under the table.

"Ouch. Okay, I probably deserved that."

She trained her dark eyes on Parker and repeated, "Well, what are your intentions?"

Jenna heard their exchange from inside and as embarrassing as it would have been if she were sitting there, from her vantage point, she was rather enjoying the show. Also, the anticipation of his answer was killing her.

Parker glanced nervously at the sliding door then back at Jenna's best friend. He knew his answer mattered and that it was too soon for a complete declaration, so he measured his reply. "My intention is to see this through and hopefully, in the end…Well, who knows what'll happen. Jenna has some say in this too."

Jenna instantly began analyzing his words. What did he mean when he said, "hopefully, in the end?" She didn't have time to consider it further as the buzzer went off, announcing the frittata was done.

"Hey V," she called.

"Yep," Veronica replied.

"Will you give me a hand?"

"Coming."

Veronica stood and chided the men, "You two just sit there looking pretty."

Cameron smacked her round backside as she sauntered inside.

"What do you need me to do?" Veronica asked as she came through the doorway.

"Um, here, set the table," Jenna said as she slid a stack of dishware across the island.

Veronica carried the plates to the table and distributed them on the already placed straw mats. Her thoughts were far from the task and instead, she thought of Cameron and the way her body betrayed her in his presence. She shook her head as she set the last fork and Jenna asked, "What, V?"

She looked up, "What? What?"

"You're shaking your head," Jenna hissed.

"I didn't realize."

Jenna sensed Veronica's struggle, "Are you okay?"

Veronica put an easy smile on her face. It didn't reach her eyes. "I'm good, too good. You?"

Jenna's heart raced and her eyes bore through the glass, settling on Parker. His golden hair was still mussed from their hasty morning tussle. What had come over her? She didn't expect things to move so quickly, but something happened when he touched her. Curiosity and pent up yearning had taken over and she'd wanted to go all the way. It was that simple. "I think I'm good."

"Good. Good. Everyone's good," Veronica said rapidly.

Jenna's attention was piqued, but Cameron's arrival in the doorway halted their chat. "I can smell it from outside."

Ding. The buzzer went off. "Nice timing, Cameron. It's just about ready."

Parker walked inside the house and toward Jenna. She couldn't make eye contact but her tell-tale body swayed toward him like a house plant to a southern window. She smoothly cut the frittata as Parker pulled the salad from the refrigerator. "Um, the serving spoons are…"

Parker slid the utensils from the edge of the counter, "Got em."

She wouldn't put weight into every little thing, she told herself, but she couldn't help it. They fit. If anything came out of their steamy morning, it was that fact. Collecting the pan, she brought it to the table. "Who's ready?"

Cameron rubbed his hands together like a mouse contemplating a morsel. "Must be all the fresh air and morning exercise," he smiled broadly.

Veronica took a seat beside him and Jenna served her. "Cameron, please take some salad," she gestured toward the bowl and added a wedge of frittata to his plate.

With Parker's and her plates filled, Jenna took her seat. Parker brought a fresh bottle of bubbly to the table and filled the glasses. "This looks delicious. Thank you, Jenna."

Veronica and Cameron tapped glasses and said, "Cheers."

The meal passed with the leisure of vacation but the nerves of budding romance. Their proximity left no room to ponder the meaning and costs of their earlier actions.

Food was pushed around by the ladies while the men ate voraciously and found common ground as they talked of the current commercial real estate situation.

Veronica and Jenna hatched a plan for the day. Veronica spoke up, "Do you guys want to go into town, check out the shops, and get groceries for dinner?

Jenna added, "I saw there's a pretty nice gas grill outside. Cookout tonight?"

Parker dropped his napkin on his plate and stood. "That works for me." He collected Jenna's dish and headed toward the kitchen.

Cameron followed his lead, taking his plate in hand and then Veronica's. "Love me some barbeque," he chuckled, "and it is so fitting for pretend Christmas Eve dinner."

The girls looked at one another. Veronica smiled oddly, "Yes, tomorrow is our early Christmas celebration! How could we forget?"

Cameron crossed the room and plucked the salad bowl from the table. "And do I have a surprise for you."

Veronica's eyes lifted and her helplessness was evident. She was falling in love with him again, or maybe she never fell completely out of love with him. Whatever it was, it shone from her like an aura. "That's so sweet." She said it as chastely as a child.

Jenna sipped from her glass and let the slug of dry wine soothe her concerns for her best friend and herself. Dating was supposed to be fun and yes, it involved risk, but no one was going to die, herself included. She knew she needed to chill out.

Parker returned to stand beside the table. "I think that's about it for cleanup."

She looked up, "Thank you for doing that."

"No problem. Thanks for cooking. Should we call Troy and let him know we're about ready?"

"Yep," Veronica jumped from her seat and burst toward the bedroom, "ready in ten."

Jenna stood, "I'd better keep her on track."

Parker and Cameron watched the ladies retreat. Each wore the grin of a satisfied man.

"Beer?" Cameron asked Parker.

"Do you think we've got time?"

Cameron snickered, "What is it she says when she's running late…?" He rubbed his chin before opening the refrigerator and extracting two beers, "Oh, yeah, 'Beautiful things never hurry.' I think we've got time."

———

"THE ANGEL and Ms. Claus have arrived," announced Veronica as she and Jenna returned.

They looked resplendent and opposite. Jenna wore cream tights under a lined poncho in gold and cream with tawny colored booties. Veronica was in black pants with a brilliant red turtleneck and matching coat with black knee-high boots.

"You both look perfect," said Parker.

"Yes, you do. Let's go," Cameron said and jumped for the door.

Troy stood at the back of the SUV. "Good morning," he called as they approached.

"Morning," they chuckled. It was late, but technically still morning when they finally set out.

Troy pulled into a public parking lot just behind the quaint streets of downtown Bend. "I'll meet you back here at 4 p.m.," he said as they exited the vehicle.

"Thanks, Troy," Veronica said and they walked away.

An early snow season was to thank for the blanket of white that muted the otherwise buzzing town. Shops were filled with people and the walkways thrived as window shoppers sipped steaming beverages. It was five days before Christmas and many were still searching for the perfect gift, the girls included.

"Hey," she called to the group, "Jenna and I have a little solo shopping to do. Why don't we split up and meet you boys here," she gestured toward a cozy looking pub, "at 2 p.m.?"

Cameron nodded and Parker agreed, "Sure, we'll see you girls in a while." He pecked Jenna's cheek as if it were natural and Cameron followed his lead. Veronica narrowed her eyes at the gesture, but said nothing.

"Farewell my sweet," he chided and the men continued down the road.

After a beat, Veronica took command, "Let's go in here."

Their entrance into the combination bookstore and gift shop was announced by a chime. "Welcome in ladies," called a merry woman from the cash register.

"Thank you," Jenna replied as Veronica began inspecting the wares.

The store was a catchall of sorts. There was art, sculptures, books, leather goods, and even some fancy weapons. Veronica walked toward a wall display and studied tiny sculptures of warriors in different poses and her mind wandered to the pose she'd struck in the woods with Cameron that morning. Desire for a rematch swept over her and she had to exhale to release the tension.

Jenna absently scanned a coffee table book about Pacific Northwest architecture. Her mind was on the unbelievably forward move she'd made with Parker. She smiled and admitted silently that it was great. Her excitement was dampened by her concerns about work but she knew there was no turning back.

"So…" Veronica drawled, "how was your alone time with Parker this morning? Did you have a nice walk?"

Jenna cleared her throat. Eyes glued to the book, she replied, "We did. Saw a fine buck for a half-second before he vanished into the brush. How'd things go with you after Cameron carried you into the woods?"

Veronica wasn't ready to tell her friend all of what happened, so she gave her the most important part, "We found a waterfall. I'll take you there tomorrow before we leave."

"Neat," Jenna replied but secretly she felt like a ho. If Veronica, who already knew Cameron intimately, could resist temptation, what was her problem? The second Parker kissed her, she practically pulled him back to the empty house. No, she wouldn't admit how forward she'd been. V would never let her live it down. "Did you have fun then?"

Veronica couldn't stop the smile from forming on her lips, "We did."

Jenna accused, "You're being vague."

"I'm not. I've answered your questions. It was only an hour, give or take. Would you like a moment by moment replay?"

She replied miffed, "No, forget it. What are you getting Cameron for our Christmas?"

Veronica shook her head as they moved through the shop. "I've been thinking about this endlessly and I still don't have an idea. What about you?"

"It just came to me," Jenna replied. "I saw a spice store down the way. I'd like to see what they have."

Veronica looked quizzically at Jenna. "Spices?"

Jenna shook her head, "You wouldn't understand."

"Oh, I understand. Do you?"

"What do you mean?"

"Have you ever heard anyone wake up on Christmas morning and say, "Oh, thank you! I was hoping for some paprika this year?"

Jenna shook her head in silence.

"Hey, look at this." Veronica leaned over a glass case inside of which was a replica of the "Lewis and Clark" compass.

"Wow, that's different and telling. To point him in the right direction so he'll always find his way home."

Veronica, who was usually assured, bit her bottom lip. "Do you think it's too much?"

Jenna watched the turf war of love and fear cross her friend's eyes. She worried for her too but said, "I think it is the exact perfect gift for the occasion. He's going to cherish it always."

Veronica replied drably, "Wow, way to make me feel like a jerk."

Jenna smiled, "What do you mean?"

"You know. I gave you a hard time about buying Parker spices and you're being so supportive about the compass."

"That's because you don't understand what I'm thinking of giving Parker. Ring that up and let's move on. You'll see I'm not far behind you on things."

Veronica studied her friend. Her cheeks were flushed and her eyes bright from the mimosas and the morning's events. She could tell something big was happening between Parker and Jenna and she was glad. Something told her he'd make a great third wheel.

They hurried through the transaction and gift-wrapping options and made their way along the snow-dappled sidewalk toward the spice shop. They opened the door to sensory overload, assaulted by aromas of mint, garlic, oregano, pepper, citrus, and ginger that wafted from glass jars upon wide shelves. "Hello, ladies. Feel free to browse.

The spices are alphabetized and I'm happy to get jars down for you to smell a sample."

"Thank you," Jenna called.

Veronica stalked around the space and gravitated toward a table with candles. "This? Is this what you had in mind for Parker?"

Jenna shook her head and replied, "It wasn't on the list, but it's a good add. Thanks, V."

Veronica watched her friend make a beeline for the spices. She stood a little taller as she looked at the labels. "Something particular you're trying to find?" the shop-keeper inquired.

"Actually, yes. Do you have saffron?"

The woman smiled, "I certainly do." She moved a ladder to reach the jar upon a higher shelf. "If you like saffron, you may enjoy this great book, *The Saffron Tales*. I've got it in stock over there. Great recipes and I love the narrator."

"Wow, that's perfect. I'll take both, please."

"Gift wrap?"

"Yes, thank you."

Veronica nudged Jenna. "You're giving him a spice and a cook book for Christmas?"

Jenna chuckled, "It's not the gift, it's what I'll write inside the book when I give it to him."

She breathed, "What? What are you going to write inside?" She was relentless, throwing one corny line out after the next. "Let's spice things up? Want to play with fire? Cook-off?"

Jenna took it in stride as she and handed her credit card over to pay for the gift.

CAMERON AND PARKER ambled along awkwardly as they peered into shop windows hoping for inspiration.

"Look," Cameron said, "a jewelry shop. If we can't find something in there, we have problems."

Parker nodded and wondered if a gift of jewelry was premature. He didn't want to scare Jenna. Then he thought of their morning together and all reservations vanished. "Good call."

They entered the micro shop and a kindly looking man greeted them. "Welcome in. Can I help you find anything?"

Parker replied, "We're looking for gifts for our…"

Cameron nearly choked out the word that Parker couldn't, "girlfriends."

The man's light eyes twinkled as he asked, "It's new then? The romance?"

Parker managed, "Yes, new. Just getting started."

Cameron made a grumbling sound.

"Well, there are some great items in this case here. Care to take a look?" The men stepped forward deliberately with a kind of reverence normally saved for a bride's march. "I'm David, by the way."

"I'm Parker and this is Cameron. He and his girl are getting back together after five years. My thing is new." As the details spewed from his mouth, Parker wondered why was he so nervous and why he was telling the shopkeeper their status.

David's eyes crinkled nearly shut as he moved toward the end of the glass case. "I have just the thing for both of you."

Cameron and Parker waited as the man took a black velvet tray from a shelf and slid the door to the case open. He removed a shiny bobble and placed it on the tray, then moved to the other end of the case and plucked a small jewelry box, setting it next to the other piece. The items gleamed from the counter as David assigned the treasures. His gnarled hands held the delicate jewelry box containing two tiny golden earrings, "This is for your friend," he said his name slowly as if doubting himself, "Cameron. Daffodils are a symbol of new beginnings. If you're starting over, this will make a wonderful statement."

Cameron took the box and examined the tiny flowers.

"And for you, Parker, the pine tree symbolizes longevity and virtue. This pendant will be perfect for you."

Parker held the shiny silver chain and clasped the feather-light tree to study the detail. His lips curved slightly as he thought of giving it to her.

Cameron choked, "I feel like we've been sharked by a combo jewelry salesman and fortune teller. It's safe to say we'll take them. Can you gift wrap?"

The man's eyes held Cameron's for a moment but he remained silent. He peered next at Parker, who seemed happy with the choice. David cleared his throat but said nothing.

Parker met his eyes, "I like this a lot. Is there a chance you have a small eagle pendant to add to it?"

David raised a finger to the sky and exclaimed, "I have just the thing." He scurried to the other side of the store, and opened the cabinet. In a blink with delicate golden eagle with diamond chip eyes. He spoke in hushed tones, "The eagle represents honesty, truth, principles, and the courage to look ahead."

Parker touched the miniature bird with sparkling eyes and thought of Jenna's expression as she admired the one they'd seen soaring above them that morning. He knew it was an important day and this was an important gift. "Thank you. I'll take them."

After paying for their respective presents and waiting

for gift wrap, the guys were out of things to do. "Should we head to the pub early?" Cameron suggested.

Parker was at ease now that he'd found the right present for Jenna. "Sure, may as well keep the buzz going."

Cameron patted his shoulder heartily, "I could tell we were going to be friends."

They backtracked in that direction as Cameron's phone buzzed. He fished it from his pocket and after seeing who it was he replaced it. Parker didn't mean to look, but he got a glimpse and he thought the Caller ID said, Kyra. Wasn't that the name of the girl from his past? He hoped not for Veronica's sake. He knew he should keep his nose out of it, but he couldn't stop himself. "What's the matter? Didn't want to take the call?"

Cameron huffed, "It's not the right time, as usual."

"What's not?" Parker pressed.

"My friend Kyra has the worst timing. We haven't talked in weeks, and now as I'm trying to get back with V, she's touching base."

Cameron opened the door to the pub and gestured for Parker to go first. "There's a table by the bar. Let's grab that," he said and walked that direction.

They sat and were greeted by the bartender. "What'll it be guys?"

Cameron spoke up, "IPA for me."

Parker agreed, "Same."

Now that their drinks were ordered, Parker was back on the subject. He decided to play coy, "I'm confused, why would your friend calling you bother Veronica?"

Cameron inhaled, "We used to date and when Veronica and I broke up, Kyra and I got back together for a while."

"Do you still see each other?"

"No. Not for a long time anyway. We're friends. She even knows about the Love Test match with V."

Parker sensed there was more, "You must talk often."

"I guess we do. I never thought about it."

"You going to tell Veronica?"

Cameron starred down at the table and used the bartender arriving with their beers to change topic.

BOOK, spices, and compass in hand, Veronica and Jenna rushed, side by side, out the shop door and nearly collided with their driver, Troy, who was standing on the walkway. His hands rested on his hips and with his midnight skin, he appeared to be an overlay against the snowy backdrop and fair-skinned population of Bend, Oregon.

"Troy," Jenna sputtered.

"Ladies," his face was impassive.

"Are you shopping too?" Jenna asked politely.

"No." His eyes rested on Veronica briefly. "I'll meet you later, where we agreed."

"Oh, okay," Jenna said to his retreating wall of a back, "unless you'd like to join us."

Veronica bristled as Troy turned around. "Join you?"

"Yes," Jenna chirped, "we're early to meet the guys. Want to pop in here for a quick drink while we wait it out?"

Troy wordlessly advanced toward the door to the pub and held it for them to enter. Jenna practically skipped over the threshold while Veronica shuffled and looked at her feet.

"The bar," Jenna exclaimed and took Veronica's hand. They wove through a few tables and found space at the end of the red velvet ensconced bar. There were two open chairs with room to stand.

Troy pulled the chairs back assisting Veronica first, then Jenna. "Thanks, Troy," Jenna said. "We can take turns sitting."

His baritone voice finally emerged. "No, thank you."

A pert blonde bartender arrived and asked, "What can I get you three?"

Jenna was on a roll as she ordered for all, "Three spiked mint-chocolate cocoas, please."

Troy's voice raised, "A virgin for me, please."

Veronica looked at him but said nothing.

Realizing how it sounded, he appeared embarrassed and for the first time, human, as he stammered, "I'm driving."

"How do you like being a driver?" Jenna asked.

"It fills the time."

His brevity was beginning to peeve Veronica as evidenced by the half eye roll she cast in his direction.

Jenna, who was accustomed to working with gruff personalities, continued questioning him. "What else do you do to fill the time?"

"I'm in the Reserves."

She drilled, "What branch?"

"Navy."

"What's your job?"

His voice lowered, "Master at Arms."

Veronica's brows rose but she said nothing.

"Impressive." Jenna replied, "Though there's not much water in Portland."

"I go north for my weekends in."

Her left field question stunned them all, "And why were you lingering outside the shop we were in?"

"Here you go, kids." The bartender placed three mugs

on the counter. "This one," she gestured to one with a red candy cane, "is the virgin."

Jenna raised her drink to toast, "Here's to the Love Test."

Veronica snatched her mug from the gleaming wooden bar and sipped unceremoniously. Troy took a tentative sip and when he set his cup down, Veronica and Jenna couldn't hold their laughter in. His upper lip was covered in cream from the drink.

Troy's unsettling eyes met Veronica's and it silenced them both. It was as if he'd pinned her to her chair. Jenna noticed the change in energy and as much as she wanted to watch, she knew it was time for a retreat. She quietly placed her mug on the counter and backed away from their trancelike eye lock, making her way toward the ladies room. They didn't break while she was in sight.

"Are you in love with him?" Troy's voice was grave despite the cream against his mouth.

Veronica was shocked and pleased. The sizzling pull she'd noticed the first time she saw him wasn't in her head. "I was once."

"Love doesn't go."

His words made an impact. She couldn't help but think about how Cameron had walked out of her life those years ago. As much as she wanted to put it behind her, the thread of doubt was easy to tug. It's probably why she snapped a reply, "Who said it's gone?"

Troy took a cocktail napkin from the table, dabbed his mouth and replied, "I apologize for overstepping. I'll meet you all at the parking lot later." He pulled some bills from his pocket and placed them on the bar before walking out.

Veronica stared as he walked out and Jenna snuck up from behind. "Boo," Jenna whispered near her ear.

Veronica turned around and Jenna searched her face. "What is happening?" Jenna asked.

"I don't know," Veronica replied and took a slug of cocoa.

"He's intense." Jenna said.

"That's for sure."

"You like it, don't you?"

Veronica ran her finger around the rim of the mug and after a beat replied, "I'm here for Cameron, to see what could have been, and maybe should have been if only I weren't too afraid. I won't deny there's"—she paused and flitted her lashes snottily—"something between Troy and I, but it could just be me sabotaging things again before they get too serious."

Jenna shrieked, "Again? What do you mean again?"

"You know how guarded I can be. I blew it back then. Cameron told me he loved me and I...I blanked. It wasn't long after that he left."

"I can't believe you're blaming yourself for his decision to move out of state and in with his ex-girlfriend."

"I'm not blaming myself, but I've finally seen the other side of it. I held back. I was in love with him, but I didn't tell him. I was afraid he'd leave me."

"And now? How do you feel about him today?"

Veronica puzzled. Was she ready to dive back into something with the man from her past? Could they make it work this time? Her voice was small as she asked, "Is it okay if we talk about something else for a while?"

Jenna knew when to back off. "Sure." She got the attention of their bartender. "Can we have two shots of Fireball please?"

"Coming right up."

THEIR DINNER of barbequed chicken and steaks was winding down. Parker and Cameron cleared the plates as Jenna poured highballs to go with the assortment of chocolates the girls insisted upon for dessert. Veronica had taken the liberty of opening each bar, creating mini piles of chocolate with labels, and arranging them on a cutting board. In the background the Christmas tree sparkled, flanked by the colorful gifts they'd brought to exchange the following morning.

As Veronica carried the board to the living room, the lights went out. "Woah," said Parker from the kitchen.

"What's happening?" asked Jenna as she found her way back from the restroom. Thankfully they'd started a fire so the room wasn't pitch dark.

"I guess the power went out," said Cameron.

"What do we do?" asked Veronica.

"Sit by the fire," he replied.

"I'll text Troy, so he knows," Parker said.

Jenna shot Veronica a look as she pulled some throw pillows from the couch and tossed them on the floor around the coffee table. "This is kind of like camping, but indoors," she said.

Parker joined them, taking the pillow by Jenna. "Troy texted me back. His power is out too. He's calling the electric company, but from the look of it, the neighborhood has gone dark. The storm must have blown a transformer or something."

Cameron chimed as he added some logs to the fire, "Well, the good news is we have plenty of wood."

"What should we do now?" Jenna asked.

"I have an idea," Veronica replied. "Why don't we play 'Never Have I Ever.'"

"What's that?" Cameron asked.

Parker chuckled.

Veronica continued, "It's a drinking game. I'll start by tell you something I've never done and if you've done it, you have to drink. Never have I ever spent a night in jail."

To the women's surprise, both Cameron and Parker picked up their glasses and took a drink.

Jenna's brows rose as she demanded, "You two better start talking."

Parker chuckled. "When I was fifteen, a few buddies and I went to a concert at the Rose Garden. We were drinking before and none of us could handle our liquor. We saw a girl I knew from school and when I went to hug her, I missed and fell to the ground. This caught the attention of a couple of security guards. They walked toward me and my friends ran. The rest you can probably figure out."

Jenna was curious, "Did you get into trouble with your parents?"

Parker shook his head in remembrance, "Dad took it okay, but my Mom was beside herself. I was grounded for a month after and I had to go to this remediation program where they showed me these pictures of alcohol-related car accidents. I guess it worked because I never drink and drive."

Veronica remained quiet as Jenna continued the questioning. "What about you, Cameron? Why did you spend the night in jail?"

"I got a DUI when I was eighteen. Lost my license for a year and I had to pay over ten-thousand dollars in fines, plus I took the same class Parker mentioned."

Jenna chided, "Obviously it worked because here we are playing a drinking game with the former jailbirds."

Veronica laughed and said, "Your turn, Jenna."

She blurted, "Never have I ever cheated on a boyfriend/girlfriend."

The room went silent as Cameron picked up glass and took a drink. After an awkward pause, he replied, "I was young."

No one dared to ask what happened. Veronica stood and said, "I need the restroom."

Cameron was right behind her, leaving Parker and Jenna on their own. "Seems like something is brewing between them," Parker said.

"Yeah, something is," Jenna replied with concern.

He scooted over, put his hands on her shoulders, and in a quiet voice said, "Turn around."

She moved so her back was to him and melted into his kneading hands.

"You're tight," he commented.

"Always. I think I was born that way."

"From what I can tell, you were born perfect."

Jenna turned around and placed a hand on Parker's cheek, "That makes two of us."

———

VERONICA STOOD in the darkened bathroom—lit only by moonlight that filtered through the skylight above—having a conversation with herself. She knew it was just a game and what Cameron did before he knew her didn't matter. A lot of people make mistakes like that, especially when they're young. Still, she couldn't help but wonder if it was a pattern for him. If maybe he didn't want a committed relationship and that's why he was swayed when his ex came calling. Her earlier conversation with Jenna boiled up. As much as she wanted to share responsibility for her part in her and Cameron's breakup those years ago, she wasn't the one who left abruptly.

His knock at the door interrupted her thoughts. "V, you okay?"

"I'll be out in a minute." She turned on the tap and splashed cool water on her cheeks. She didn't need to wash away the tears because she hadn't cried since the day her mother dropped her off with her aunt and never returned.

As she opened the door, Cameron approached. His face was shadowed under the grainy light. "Hey," he said.

Veronica cleared her throat, "What's up?"

"Nothing, I wanted to check on you. Are you upset with me?"

Anger wasn't the emotion that bubbled up with his admission. It wasn't jealousy either. It was insecurity and fear of abandonment. She'd had enough therapy over the years to understand her reactions. Could she explain it to Cameron? "No, I'm not upset with you." It was partially true.

"Well, you left the room pretty fast after that last question."

She inhaled sharply and lied. "I needed the restroom."

He closed the distance between them in the hallway and reached to hug her. Veronica bristled and found an escape. "Let's get back to the game."

Cameron ran his hands through his dark hair in frustration. "V, I'm sorry. I can't apologize enough for what happened back then. All I can do is show you how different I am now."

She nodded almost imperceptibly. The shell that she'd spent decades strengthening to protect her from those long-known feelings of betrayal surrounded her again. "I'm not upset. I'll see you out there," she said and walked toward the living room.

PARKER AND JENNA were spooning and asleep on the floor and Cameron snored softly at one end of the sofa, as Veronica lay awake thinking about the day. A cold wisp of air filled the room when the front door opened quietly. A moment later, Troy entered the living room. He carried two small gift bags as he tiptoed toward the unlit Christmas tree. After setting them beneath it, he crossed the room to the dwindling fire and added more wood. He turned and Veronica closed her eyes. She didn't hear him approach, but felt the weight of the blanket as he pulled it up to her shoulders. She opened her eyes then. They spoke volumes in the briefest of glances. A moment later, he was gone. As the door shut, an unexplained lone tear streamed down her cheek.

———

THE LIGHTS WERE an abrupt wake-up call that roused the couples. It was their faux Christmas morning and Jenna was the first to sit up. Veronica and she made eye contact. "Mornin'," Jenna said.

Veronica grumbled, "Mornin'."

"Merry Christmas," Cameron said as he sat up. His thick hair was smashed at the side.

From his position on the floor, Parker wrapped his arms around Jenna's waist. "How'd everyone sleep?"

Cameron rose and started to stretch, "Like a baby."

Jenna's heart fluttered as she looked at Parker, "I slept great."

"Me too," he agreed.

Cameron walked to Veronica's end of the couch and kissed her on the forehead. "Merry Christmas."

She replied, "Merry Christmas."

"I'm making breakfast," he exclaimed.

Parker replied, "I'll start the coffee." Before he headed for the kitchen, he touched Jenna's cheek. His eyes shined with a tenderness that made her stomach drop.

Veronica got up and announced, "We'll freshen up and see you boys in a few." She headed toward their bedroom with Jenna closely behind.

Once inside, Jenna shut the door and sat on the bed watching her best friend rifle through her suitcase. "V."

Veronica didn't respond.

She persisted, "Veronica."

She glanced over her shoulder but didn't speak.

"Talk to me."

"About?" She played dumb which they both knew was pointless.

Jenna demanded. "Really?"

"What do you want me to say?"

Jenna understood there would be no getting through to Veronica in this moment. "When you're ready to talk, you know I'm here."

Veronica's expression was impassive. "I'm going to get in the shower."

As Veronica left the room, Jenna sunk back onto the bed and was overwhelmed by a feeling of joy, followed closely by guilt. She was falling for Parker and it seemed mutual. He was the perfect combination of strong and kind and Jenna sensed they were on the same page. Even with the work obstacle they'd have to face, she was almost certain they were in it together. Veronica deserved the same reciprocity and she wondered if Cameron was capable.

THE GIRLS RETURNED to the living room to find Cameron and Parker busy in the kitchen. Cameron pulled bacon from the oven as Cameron finished setting the table. From the looks of their damp hair, both had showered and still managed to make breakfast.

Cameron crossed the room to Veronica. "Your first present is ready. Won't you take a seat?" He walked to the table and held a chair for her to sit.

Parker went for the coffee pot and filled everyone's mugs.

"Have a seat, buddy," Cameron said as he arrived at the table with a pan.

Starting with Veronica, he placed some strange-looking eggs on their plates. Parker and Jenna shared a look as they studied the meal.

Veronica's eyes narrowed and her jaw clenched.

Cameron sat and said, "Merry Christmas everyone. I know these eggs look a bit off, but Veronica and I can attest, they taste better than they look."

Veronica studied her plate. The eggs were an omelet of chocolate chip cookies and were covered with a layer of powdered sugar and butter. From the seat to her left, Cameron put a hand on hers and said, "Surprise."

His gesture touched her deeply. Her mind wandered back to that night they spent in the crappy apartment and a time when things were clear. She responded simply, "Thank you, Cameron."

He smiled broadly, "Let's just hope it's as good as we remember."

Parker and Jenna tentatively raised their forks.

"Wow," Jenna said after she took a bite, "interesting."

Parker agreed, "Yeah, unique."

Veronica took a bite of her eggs and so did Cameron. The flavor was unexpected: Crunchy, melty cookies were dispersed into the fluffy eggs and the sugar that coated their lips.

"I have to ask," said Parker, "were you guys high when you came up with this recipe?"

Cameron chuckled, "There may have been a puff or two involved. Since the cupboards were bare except for a package of Chips Ahoy cookies and a few eggs, we had to improvise. What do you think?"

Parker laughed.

Jenna studied her normally boisterous friend. She empathized with her desire to believe in Cameron. "Very sweet, Cameron, on two levels."

"Thanks, Jenna."

While no one cleaned their plates, they shared a meal that once meant love. Breakfast was winding down and the women did the dishes. Parker sipped at his coffee and asked, "Is it time for presents yet?"

"Sure," Jenna replied as she wiped her hands on a towel.

They made their way toward the tree and Parker took the lead. "Hey, look at this, there are a couple of presents for Veronica and Jenna." He picked each bag up and handed them to the girls.

The shiny red gift bags were identical except for the name tags. Veronica hesitated to open hers, since after last night she knew they were from Troy.

Jenna excitedly emptied the contents and unwrapped them from the glittery tissue paper. Inside was a red thermos, a metal container with mint-chocolate cocoa powder and a bottle of peppermint schnapps. Her eyes met Veronica's.

"Who is that from?" Parker asked.

Jenna answered casually though she understood the meaning behind the gift. "I'm pretty sure they're from

Troy. We bumped into him on the street yesterday and since we'd finished our shopping early, the three of us had hot chocolate."

Cameron looked at Veronica who had yet to open hers. "Is it the same?" He asked unaware of the underlying message.

She pulled the items from inside and they were identical to what Jenna's bag held, only there was a small card at the bottom of her bag. She left it unopened as she replaced the contents into the bag. "Yep, it's the same," she announced.

"Well, that was thoughtful of him," Parker said.

"Yeah," Veronica mumbled.

"Let's get you boys something to open," Jenna said.

She handed one present to Cameron and the other to Parker.

Parker could hardly contain himself as he tore into the first miniature present. His large fingers struggled to grasp the wrapping paper that surrounded the cube-like gift. With the paper off, Parker exclaimed, "Saffron! Thank you."

"That's not all," Jenna said, as she gestured toward the other gift. "They go together."

He tore through the pine tree wrap and uncovered the book. "What's this? *The Saffron Tales...*" he said as he opened the cover.

Jenna's breath held as he read her inscription.

PARKER,

It seems that you and saffron are equally rare. After the Love Test is over, I'd like to share another cooking session with you. Here's to the future.

xo,

Jenna

WITHOUT A WORD, he leaned over and pulled Jenna into a kiss. They were lost for a moment as Cameron and Veronica looked on. When they managed to pull apart, Jenna said, "You next, Cameron."

He held the small red package and pulled at the sides, tearing the paper and exposing a leather box with a lid. He removed the lid to find the compass resting against a pillow of brown silk. Veronica had taped a small message to the underside of the cover.

CAMERON,
   To point you in the right direction.
   Merry Christmas,
   V

HE REMOVED the compass from the box and held it up to examine. His gaze turned to Veronica and he said, "Thank you, V. I love it." He got to his feet and took a package from beneath the tree. "This is for you."

She unwrapped the gift and felt a pang of nerves as she faced the small leather box. "Open it," he pressed.

The lid opened with a snap and she was relieved to find a dainty pair of earrings inside. Cameron said, "They're daffodils, a symbol of new beginnings."

Veronica's sentiments collided between the bygone and present. They had history and though some of it was bad, really bad, most of it was great. Before he moved, they'd never even had an argument. For five years, she'd longed to reclaim the past and now that he was here, she felt trepidation, but why? Until Troy ruffled her feathers, she was on track. "They're lovely, Cameron. Thank you so much." She got onto her knees and kissed his cheek.

"You're welcome," he said and he held her wrist, keeping her in place. His eyes pleaded, as if he knew she was pulling away.

She kissed him on the cheek once more as Parker cleared his throat. "There's one more gift," he said and handed Jenna a box.

"Thank you, Parker," she replied as she accepted the package. Within seconds, she'd torn through the snowflake-covered paper and found her own leather box inside. She pushed open the lid and her breath caught as she studied the necklace and tiny pendants. Inside the box was a note.

JENNA,

The pine tree symbolizes longevity and virtue, while the eagle represents the courage to look ahead.

I'm looking forward,
Parker

JENNA'S EYES misted as she touched the miniature figures that held so much meaning. "Here," Parker said, "let me put it on for you."

She turned so he could affix the chain and when she faced him, he bowled her over with his comment. "After standing together on the deck yesterday, surrounded by pines and watching you watch that eagle, I knew this was the perfect gift. Do you like it?"

She rasped, "It's beautiful. Thank you, Parker."

Their kiss sealed the moment and a second later, Parker's phone buzzed. He took it from the table and announced, "Guys, Love Test has a surprise for us. Troy sent a message asking that we be ready to leave in an hour."

THEY DROVE a short distance and stopped at a regional airport. One small building and a traffic control tower greeted them as Troy circled the car to help them out. "Go ahead into the building," he said.

The group entered the small airport, complete with drop-tile ceilings and 1970s furnishings. Troy wasn't far behind. "Give me a minute," he said and made his way to the counter. After conferring with the attendant, he called, "This way."

They followed him to a set of double doors and walked outside as he held the door. "We're down on the end," he announced and walked purposefully in front.

Arriving at the final gate, he marched along the painted white walkway toward a sleek, black helicopter. He opened the door and gestured for the group to enter. "Welcome to the Panther," he said with a grin on his face.

This was the first time Veronica had seen him smile and it did things to her she couldn't admit, even to herself.

As they filed inside, the women took the window seats and the guys settled into the two center spots. Troy made the rounds assuring that they were correctly secured into their restraints and giving each a headset. "I've never been in a helicopter before," Jenna said as he checked her connections.

"Me neither," agreed Parker.

"That makes three," Cameron confirmed.

When Troy made it to Veronica, he asked, "And you, Veronica? Have you flown on a helicopter?"

Hearing him say her name sent chills down her spine. She shook her head, no, but said nothing. That was when she remembered the unread note at the bottom of his gift to her.

He smiled again and her stomach dropped. "It's going to be loud, so keep your headsets on. Let's get going," he said as he ducked and settled himself into the front seat.

Cameron asked, "You're our pilot?"

Troy nodded as he began checking dials and flipping switches.

"Limos and helicopters?" Cameron continued, "What else can you drive?"

Troy's voice was deep as he replied, "Tanks."

"Impressive," Cameron said.

Jenna's eyes met Veronica's.

Troy started a conversation with the control tower and after their exchange they began hovering. Troy's voice tickled Veronica's ears as he shared, "The flight to Portland will take under an hour. Enjoy the view, everyone."

Veronica's insides felt hectic and she knew it wasn't only because of the helicopter's strange motion. The ground beneath shrank as they rose above the buildings and lurched forward. The snow covered high-desert, surrounded by mountainous peaks, unfolded under Troy's capable hands. As enthralling as the view was, Veronica couldn't help by steal a glance at Troy from time to time. He appeared in his element and perfectly in command of the tiny vessel.

"Look," Parker said, "The Three Sisters."

Cameron put his hand on Veronica's knee, "Incredible."

His hand on her leg should have been welcome, but she had to stop herself from removing it. Then she remembered his thoughtful gesture of making their special breakfast and his words as he gave her the earrings.

Parker and Jenna snuggled together. They alternated between staring out the window and into each other's eyes.

The mainly barren land was covered in a blanket of white. Highway 20 stood as a dark beacon against the frosty surroundings. The Deschutes River carved a path in the icy backdrop and paralleled their way home.

After a time, Troy spoke. "We're coming up on Mt. Hood. I'll circle so you can get a better view."

Veronica's stomach dropped as the helicopter shifted slightly to one side, giving her an even better view of the glacier. The mountain was dotted with tiny moving skiers and snowboarders making their descent down the powdered surface. The sprawling rock lodge came into view as they turned.

"This is amazing, Troy," Jenna announced. "Thank you."

"Nah," he said, "don't thank me. This is all from the man upstairs."

Veronica perked at his words. Her faith had been a saving grace during so many difficult life experiences. She appreciated devotion in others, though she didn't demand it.

The helicopter straightened and Troy asked, "Should we have a little fun?"

Parker spoke for all, "Sure!"

From the side, Veronica could see Troy smile. He straightened the helicopter and said, "Hold on." They descended and it felt like their stomachs were still above them. He maneuvered the rig until it seemed it might graze the towering evergreens. They raced above the tree-tops until Troy lifted the nose, pressing their backs to the seats.

A giggle escaped Veronica's mouth and Cameron chuckled too.

It wasn't long after that Troy announced, "We're about five minutes away from the airport."

"Aww," Jenna made her disappointment known. She wasn't ready for their fun excursion to end, nor did she want to relinquish Parker's hand.

He squeezed her fingers and said, "This weekend went by way too fast."

Cameron piped up, "Yes, it did."

Veronica trained her eyes on the impending airport and said nothing.

Troy's professionalism was evident as he negotiated with the communications tower and secured their landing position. Once on the ground, they filed out and navigated through the airport. "There is a car waiting for us," he announced.

The group traveled through the airport with Troy at the lead. Parker and Jenna held hands and swayed into each other as they went and Cameron wrapped his arm around Veronica's shoulder. They crossed the path, walking under the skybridge, and stopped by another limo.

"What's up, Troy?" asked a tall, thin man with green eyes. "How was the flight?"

"Not bad," he said as he clasped the man's hand for a shake.

"Everyone, this is my buddy, Ed. He's going to get us home."

They chimed a group greeting as Ed held the door for the couples to pile in. Ed and Troy got into their seats in the front as they navigated first to Parker's house. The car came to a stop and Troy opened the door.

Jenna got out first and said to Troy, "I'll be right back."

Troy nodded and watched the pair walk toward Parker's front door.

Parker faced Jenna. His expression reflected the happiness she thought might burst from her skin. "This weekend meant a lot to me, Jenna. I knew you were special the first time I saw you and after these past couple of days, I'm not sure how I'm going to be away from you."

His admission mirrored her feelings and it took her breath away. She didn't have time to react as his mouth took hers in the most torturously soft kiss. The scent of his mild cologne teased her nose and her pulse quickened.

They pulled apart reluctantly and Jenna said, "Until New Year's Eve."

In no time they were back on the road and en route to Cameron's house. Troy opened the door and held out his hand for Veronica to take. She liked the way it felt, which was unfortunate since she was there for Cameron. She pushed her thoughts down as Cameron jumped out behind her.

His arm once again rested on her shoulders as they moved toward his door. Without a word, Cameron pulled Veronica into his arms and smothered her with his lips. He didn't hold back and deepened the kiss. She was too in her head to enjoy it, knowing that Troy could see them. She put a hand to his chest, a silent signal to end their kiss and said, "Thank you for this weekend and for the thoughtful gifts."

Cameron's eyes held hers, "No, thank you. It was great. I can't wait until our next date."

She smiled thinly and said, "I'll see you then."

Jenna and Veronica were silent on the last few miles home. Jenna's mind was occupied by Parker. She'd made a pact with herself to not consider the work situation, if only for the weekend. Since it was still Sunday, she was free to enjoy their budding romance. Veronica wasn't as certain and though Cameron was gone, the surly powerhouse of a man who'd upset her path was in close range.

They pulled to a stop and the ladies filed out. Ed put their bags at the door and Jenna said, "Thank you, Ed." Before she sauntered into the house, she tapped Troy on the shoulder, "That helicopter ride was incredible, Troy."

"I'm glad you had fun," he replied.

Veronica was about to follow Jenna when Troy asked, "Can I talk to you for a minute?"

Jenna flashed a look over her shoulder and scurried into the house as Ed ensconced himself into the cabin of the car.

Veronica met Troy's eyes as he worried, "I apologize if I've been inappropriate. I understand that you and Cameron have history, and you were matched by the program. I hope my note didn't cross the line."

Veronica looked dismayed and her reply matched. "I haven't read the note but I'm not sure what you want from me."

Troy nodded and pursed his lips. "Maybe, once you read it, you will."

She was flabbergasted by his boldness, but held a blank expression. "Thank you for everything, Troy." Without a backward look, she found her way inside the house. The minute she closed the door, she hastily pulled the gift bag from her luggage. At the bottom was the small envelope. She removed the card from inside and read his message.

VERONICA,

People are like puzzle pieces. When they meet their match, every-thing clicks. If it doesn't easily go into place, it's not the right fit. I hope you find your counterpart. Maybe it isn't the person you were expecting.

Yours,

Troy

206-425-7878

SHE DIDN'T PAUSE for consideration and instead picked up her cell phone and composed a hasty message to Troy.

She wrote: *You don't even know me.*

It didn't take but a few seconds for his reply: *Maybe not, but I know something is between us and I think you do too.*

Troy was floored when his phone suddenly began to ring with Veronica's inbound call. Pinpricks of nerves ran along his neck as he answered, "Hello."

Her tone was tight as she demanded, "What makes you think you know anything about me, Troy?"

He cleared his throat and replied, "I know your background Veronica and I understand you. I was in foster care from the time I was nine years old. Getting out, being in control of my own destiny, nothing mattered more to me—until I saw you. I can't explain why I sense that we fit, but I do."

His words took the air out her lungs. A beat later she gasped, "I need to go."

RYAN ARRIVED on Monday evening at promptly 7 p.m. Jenna went to the door to let him in. "Hi, Ryan. It's good to see you."

He smiled, displaying his stunning dimples. "Good to see you too, Jenna."

"Come in. V is in the dining room."

He followed her down the hall until they found her. "Hey, Ryan," Veronica called in an easy tone that belied her nerves.

"Hi, Veronica."

"Have a seat," Jenna said. "Would you like something to drink?"

"No thanks. I'm good."

"Okay," Jenna said. "Do you want us both here or one at a time?"

Ryan replied, "I think it would be best to meet one on one."

"Okay, I'll go upstairs and you can start with V. Let me know when you're ready for me."

"Thanks, Jenna," said Ryan.

Ryan settled himself down and removed a notepad from his bag. "How are you feeling, Veronica?"

She twisted her fingers and made eye contact. "I'm fine. How are you?"

He didn't miss the nerves, or the heaviness in her expression. "I'm good. Should we get started?"

"Sure," she replied without inflection.

"Let's start with Bend and your faux Christmas celebration."

"Okay," she replied.

"How did it feel to wake up and spend the day with Cameron?"

Veronica contemplated his question, "It was nice. He made us a special breakfast, a recipe we came up with when we were first dating. We all exchanged gifts and he gave me a pair of earrings."

She'd answered the question without telling him anything, which in itself was telling, but Ryan couldn't surmise—as a journalist, he needed more. "What was on the menu that day?"

She gave a half-snort, half-chuckle. "Frosted eggs with Chips Ahoy."

Ryan shook his head. "Were the cookies in the eggs?"

Veronica half-smiled. "Yes. It's something we made years up ago when we were hungry and the only food in the house was eggs and cookies."

The smile should have reached her eyes, but it didn't. "It sounds like he gave that a lot of thought. Were you surprised?"

"I was."

Interviewing Veronica was almost as tough as interviewing a drug mule. Her succinct messages spoke volumes. "Did it taste as good as you remembered?"

"I'm not even sure it tasted great the first time, but it was nice of him to think of it."

"May I ask, back when you concocted this recipe, why didn't you go to the store and pick up other ingredients?"

Veronica's expression went wistful. "We didn't want to leave the house. It was our little bubble."

"So, Cameron's breakfast was a strong reminder of the connection you once had."

"It was."

"Did that breakfast reignite those feelings of wanting to stay inside your bubble?"

For the first time since they'd started the interview, Veronica met Ryan's gaze. "Things are different now. I don't need a bubble anymore."

"Did you need it back then?"

"I wanted it."

Ryan considered her comment and decided it was time to change his line of questioning. "With Christmas coming in the next few days, how do you feel knowing you won't see Cameron on the actual day?"

The air between them was heavy and she finally

replied, "I...Well, it's part of the deal, so I haven't given it a lot of thought. I know the rules."

Her evasion was as transparent as her doubts. "At the start of the Love Test, you committed to remain open-minded until the decision date. Are you still planning to continue?"

She pursed her lips and inhaled audibly. "I'll see it through until the end."

The way she said "until the end" perked Ryan's attention. "How do you feel about the prospect of being together when this is over?"

Her reply was almost a justification, "For five years I've wished things turned out differently between Cameron and me. Now I realize it was both of us who let it go..."

She didn't answer his question but from the downcast expression she held, Ryan couldn't bring himself to push her further. "Thank you, Veronica. I appreciate you speaking with me."

She looked up. "Are we finished?"

"One last question, if you don't mind."

"Sure," she hesitated.

"What do you think about Parker?"

For the first time since he'd arrived, Veronica smiled. "He's a sweetheart."

"Do you think he and Jenna are a good match?"

"From what I've seen, I can't imagine a better person for her."

"Why do you feel that way?"

Veronica looked almost sad as she replied, "There's an ease between them. They have a lot of respect for each other and it shows."

"Thank you, Veronica. I appreciate your sharing with me tonight."

"Of course," she replied. "I'll get Jenna."

JENNA ENTERED the room with a smile, "Here I am."

"Hi, Jenna." Ryan waited for her to sit and asked, "How are you feeling?"

"Pretty great, I have to admit."

"Oh? Is this due to your match with Parker."

Her smile was contagious. "I think so."

"How did it feel to wake up with him on your early 'Christmas morning' date?"

She toyed with the pendants that dangled on her necklace. "This is going to sound soppy, but I felt like a kid having a sleepover with her best friend. He's so easy to be around."

"That doesn't sound soppy at all. How did you spend the morning?"

"It started with Cameron making us all this funny breakfast that he and V came up with when they were first dating."

"How was it?"

Her expression went green. "It was sweet on two levels."

"So, you won't be having that again?"

She shook her head, "I hope not."

He laughed. "What else did you guys do?"

"We exchanged gifts, which was a blast."

"What did you give Parker?"

Her cheeks flushed then. "I gave him some saffron and a cookbook."

"Nice. I take it you both really enjoyed the cooking date you had."

She nodded, "We did."

"And your gift suggest that you might want to do it again. Was that your intention?"

She hesitated but only to smile. "It was."

"Did Parker give you a gift?"

Jenna proudly pushed the pendants forward. "He gave me these."

"Is that an eagle and a pine tree?"

"That's right, but it wasn't so much the gift as the meaning behind them."

"Oh?"

"Yes, he wrote this card about looking forward and that the pendants were symbolic of longevity and the courage to look ahead. He's very sweet and earnest."

"It sounds like it."

"How do you feel knowing you won't see him on the actual Christmas day?"

Her eyes went to the table then back to Ryan. "I know the rules and I'll follow them, but it's kind of a bummer."

"I understand. Have you two discussed the next steps, assuming things continue to progress? I know you have a work situation to address."

For the first time since they began, Jenna looked sad. "He tried to talk to me about it, but I asked if we could wait. I know we have to deal with it eventually, but I couldn't bring myself to tackle it just yet."

"At the start of this, you agreed to stay committed until the last date. Are you still on board?"

She nodded but looked a bit worried. "I am."

"Can I ask you what you think about Cameron and Veronica as a couple?"

Her lips went straight and for the first time since the interview started she stopped touching her necklace. "I'm not sure."

Ryan pressed. "Care to explain?"

"Well, as much as V wanted to reconcile with Cameron, she's a different person now. They both are, and

135

you can't erase their history. Some things are hard to forget."

"Did she give Cameron a present?"

"She did. It was a compass."

Ryan pondered. "That's a pretty telling token. Do you think he understood the meaning behind it?"

Jenna tilted her head to the side, "I think he did."

"Thank you for your time tonight, Jenna, and for being so candid. I wish the best for all of you."

"Thanks, Ryan. I'll walk you out."

They made it to the door and Jenna said, "Please, say hello to Lanie for us."

"I will. Goodnight, Jenna.

7

CONFETTI

The ringing phone roused Lanie from her nap on the couch. She hadn't intended to doze off, but lately, she'd been finding it harder and harder not to succumb to the exhaustion of pregnancy. "Hello?" she answered groggily.

"Hi, Lanie. This is Isabell, your realtor."

"How are you?"

"I'm doing well. Did I catch you at a good time?"

Lanie stifled a yawn and replied, "Sure."

"Great. Well, I'm calling because I've just stumbled across a home that I think you and Ryan will love."

"Oh?" Lanie leaned forward on the couch.

"It's not on the market yet, which is why I'm calling you. If you guys have time this evening, I'd love to show it to you."

"Um, I think we can manage. Ryan went for a run, but I think the rest of the day is open."

"Wonderful. I'll text you the address. Shall we say 5 p.m.?"

Lanie replied, "Sure. We'll see you then. Thanks, Isabell."

"You're welcome. I'll see you this evening."

━━━

THEY PULLED up to the curb of a lovely 1940s cottage that was situated on a hill overlooking the park and city below. The faded beige exterior was highlighted by a glowing porch light that illuminated a wrap-around porch and period windows. The home looked to be three stories, with a basement that was partially subterranean and a high peak at the roof. Behind the home was the frame of a glorious oak tree, barren of leaves against the cold January winter.

"Ryan, it's beautiful."

He said nothing but circled the car to help her out. At nearly eight months pregnant, Lanie felt like she was waddling as they took the path that led to the house. The realtor opened the door and called, "Good evening, you two."

"Hello, Isabell," said Ryan and they approached the front steps.

"Come in," she replied as she stepped back to allow them entrance.

As they crossed the threshold, Lanie felt something akin to love. There was a familiarity about the home, and a sense of welcoming she'd only experienced one other time in her life, the night she and Ryan met. The foyer faced a set of stairs and was flanked on either side by a living and dining room. Wide-plank oak floors, scarred by age and the knots of time, creaked under foot, and a cozy wood-burning fireplace popped and crackled. The original glass and crystal chandelier shined prominently in the dining room. The space was completed by built-in cabinets with glass fronts. The banister of polished wood gleamed along the painted white stairs. Without realizing it, Lanie squeezed Ryan's hand.

He looked her way but said nothing.

"First impressions?" the realtor tested.

Ryan cleared his throat and Lanie couldn't contain her interest, "Show me more."

Isabell's dark eyes crinkled at the corners as she led them through the dining room and into the large farm-style kitchen. The counters were butcher-block style and the room was U-shaped with marvelous wooden cabinets at the bottom and shelves along each wall. Toward the back was a bay window with an eating nook. The original cast iron sink remained and only a few chips of black showed through, displaying more character than wear. To the side was a back door of wood and glass.

"Can you see yourself cooking dinner in this kitchen?" Isabell asked.

Lanie smiled and her green eyes danced at the prospect. "It's a perfect kitchen."

"Let me show you the yard," Isabell stated and they followed her through the door and peered out into a wide lawn lit only by a few dim solar lights. There was a small brick patio area with a table and chairs. A trellis of sleeping rose vines edged the seating area. The lawn was wide and surrounded by ancient trees, creating a bowl of privacy.

"It's big," Ryan said.

"It is," agreed Isabell with a shiver of delight.

"Shall we take a look at the rest?"

"Yes," Lanie replied instantly.

"This way," she gestured and they circled back to the living room. On one end of the space was a wall-sized bookshelf and at the other end were windows overlooking the spacious front yard. Isabell was silently patting herself on the back for coming early and lighting the fire. As they soaked it in, she could tell by their body language that of the homes she'd shown them, this one outranked them all.

"There's a little surprise in this room." Isabell said as she walked toward the back wall that supported the stairs. "Check this out." She opened an invisible door that contained a hidden closet. "While closets are nice, this little cubby struck me as a great hideout. My kids would have loved something like this when they were small."

"Oh, that's darling," Lanie replied.

Ryan admired it as well. "That is pretty cool."

"Are you ready to head upstairs?" Isabell asked.

"Sure," said Lanie and they followed her up the steps.

"There are three nice sized bedrooms up here. The master is on your right."

The aged oak floors continued throughout and as they entered the master bedroom, a set of French doors beckoned to them. Lanie walked that direction and exclaimed, "What a view!"

"Yes," commented Isabell. "From here you can watch the sunrise over Mt. Hood."

"Wow." Ryan was also impressed.

"Why don't I leave you two for a while. Take a look around. I'll be waiting in the kitchen."

"Thank you, Isabell," Lanie said and she left them to explore the space.

"Ryan, this is pretty amazing, right?"

He nodded and agreed, "It is. She hasn't mentioned the price yet, which scares me a little."

Lanie moved as swiftly as her advanced pregnancy allowed as she pulled him into the other bedrooms. One had a view of the garden and the other of the front yard. A large family bathroom, complete with marble floors and the original cast iron tub, was situated between the rooms.

"It's gorgeous."

"It is. Let's see if we can afford it and how quickly we'd need to close escrow. We haven't even listed our places yet."

"True," Lanie said, "but they shouldn't take long to sell."

Ryan couldn't help but notice the sparkle in her eyes as she looked around. "Why don't we go down and talk to Isabell about the numbers."

They made their way back downstairs and Lanie noticed all the special details of the house. There were old double-hung windows of the finest wood and thick molding at the baseboards and ceilings. All the light plates were original and brass, even the front door seemed to be original.

"There you are," said Isabell as they entered the kitchen. "What do you think?"

Lanie replied, "It's a special house. We're a little afraid to ask how much it is."

Isabella nodded knowingly. "They want a bit more than you were hoping to spend, but I think with the proceeds from both of your homes, the numbers will pencil."

Ryan asked, "Why are they selling?"

"The owner had to move out after living here for forty years because she's having a hard time keeping up with everything, and now that she's situated with family, she's motivated."

Lanie had walked toward the kitchen window and surveyed the yard. When she turned around, Ryan was a goner. Her expression was as telling as her comment. "I love it. Can you prepare an estimate for us and give us an idea of timing?"

"I certainly can. Since tomorrow is New Year's Eve,

will Tuesday be soon enough?"

Lanie's expression flashed worried. "Will they be patient with us? We have a lot to accomplish to make it work."

"I've already given them an idea of your situation. The seller was adamant that she wanted someone who would love the house as much as she and her late husband had. Her words were, 'I hope the next people fill this home with all the love we found here.'"

Lanie's eyes teared up and she tried to make a joke, "This child inside of me is wreaking havoc on my emotions."

Isabell replied, "It was a while ago for me, but I remember. Ryan, what do you think?"

He looked from Lanie to Isabell. "I can see us making a life here and Lanie's wishes are all the incentive I need."

"Wonderful! I'll get to work on the numbers and we can meet on Tuesday to review everything."

"Thank you so much Isabell," Lanie said.

"Of course."

On the drive home, Lanie excitedly talked about the things she'd like to do to customize the house and Ryan thought that seeing the home was exactly like the first time they'd met. Life had been good before he knew her. He didn't know anything was missing, but the instant she walked into his life, he knew he would do whatever it took to be with her. Until today, giving up his home—his escape from the world—was hard to imagine. After seeing the house and especially Lanie's reaction, he knew it was where they'd raise their family.

JENNA AND VERONICA sat side by side in comfortable leather chairs. The rolling sensation eased their backs as the turbulent warm water soothed their feet. "I'm glad you pushed me to do this, V."

"You are literally the only woman I know who has to be convinced to have a pedicure," Veronica lobbed.

"Not all of us are into pampering," Jenna replied.

Veronica shook her head but said nothing.

"What color are you doing?"

Veronica held up a bottle of black polish intermixed with glitter. "Asteroid Landing is the name."

"Modern," Jenna replied.

"What about you?"

Jenna held up a bottle of nude and said, "I couldn't decide. This seems fine."

Veronica's exasperated expression matched her reply. "You can't pick that. It's New Year's Eve. Choose something more...more," she emphasized by sweeping her hands.

Jenna huffed, "Who is going to notice my feet?"

"Parker will. He hasn't seen you in weeks. He's going to notice everything."

The mention of his name caused a spike in Jenna's spirits. She was excited and nervous to see him again. With their offices closed for two weeks over the holidays, she hadn't so much as passed him in the hall since their weekend in Bend.

"Here." Veronica handed her a bottle of golden polish. "This is your color."

Jenna studied the sparkly liquid and shrugged, "Okay."

"How do you feel about tonight?" Veronica asked.

Jenna turned the bottle around and around in her hands. A smile lifted the corners of her mouth and her eyes took on a dreamy expression. "I think I'm excited."

"You think?" Veronica pressed.

"Well, there's still the work situation, which I've been denying, but I haven't been able to stop thinking about him since our last date."

"You mean you haven't been able to stop thinking about his…"

"Don't say it."

Veronica shrugged, "Don't be such a prude."

"I'm not a prude. I just don't want to boil it down to that. I'm not risking my job for sex. I like Parker."

Veronica went quiet and took a sip of her tea.

"What about you? How are you doing with everything?"

She affixed her eyes to the television that was mounted in the corner. A Spanish soap opera played on mute. The subtitles flashed across the screen explaining the fiery scene between two lovers who were in a passionate embrace. A man walked through the door to find them and the camera zoomed in on his shocked expression. "I'm good," she replied without conviction.

"Come on, V. I haven't pushed you about the letter Troy gave you or how you felt after the weekend with Cameron. You're going to see him tonight and Troy, since he's driving us. Aren't you nervous?"

Veronica didn't know how to feel and it showed in her reply. "I think I'll get a good buzz going before the night begins. That will help everything."

"V, don't forget the reason we did this. It started with a dare but deep down we both knew we were ready to find someone. You deserve to be happy and secure. I know that last part is a little harder for you…"

Veronica huffed, blowing a wisp of dark bangs with the action. "You're right. I still have some work to do, but I know it now."

Jenna shook her head. "We all have work to do, but don't let that be your crutch. You are a smart, attractive, and fun woman. You've had it harder than most, but it doesn't have to continue that way. You could find ease and you deserve to."

Veronica contemplated Jenna's words and as hard as they were to accept, she knew she'd say the same to her if things were reversed.

———

HIS KNOCK at the door landed at precisely 8 p.m. "I'll get it," Jenna yelled from the kitchen. She opened the door to Troy. "Hi, Troy."

"Hello, Jenna. You look great," he said as he studied her white and golden fitted dress. "Parker is going to lose his mind."

"Why, thank you, Troy. Come in. V is still finishing up."

He entered the house tentatively and followed her into the kitchen. "I'm pouring shots. I know you can't join us, but will you take our picture before we go?"

"Of course," he agreed as Veronica swept into the room wearing a silver and black baby doll dress. Her fit legs were enhanced by matching black platform sandals. "Veronica, you look beautiful." His eyes held hers.

She didn't want to blush, but biology betrayed her. She snapped a reply, "Thanks, Troy." She directed her question at Jenna, "Oooh, is that tequila?"

"You know it. Troy is going to take our picture before we go. Here," she said and handed Veronica a shot glass. "Let's stand by the fireplace."

Veronica followed Jenna to the living room. "Here's my phone, Troy."

He took it in hand and waited for the ladies to pose. Holding up their glasses to tap, they said, "Cheers."

Troy took the picture and studied the results. "That's a good one."

They downed their shots and Jenna said in an annoyingly happy voice, "Let's go."

Veronica knew how excited Jenna was to see Parker again. If she were honest with herself, she felt more nerves than excitement about seeing Cameron. Was she uncomfortable because of Troy's interest? Cameron had done nothing to deserve her misgivings. In fact, from all he had shown, he was trying for a fresh start. If the earrings he gave her—though not her style—were any indication, he was sincere. Still, she was distracted by Troy's alluring cologne and the way he moved with determination. He had a unique pull she found hard to resist. Her pulse quickened as they pulled up to the high-rise that was home to the Portland City Grill and the location of this evening's date.

After leaving the car at the valet, Troy escorted them up the elevator to the 30th floor and toward the check-in at the hostess station. "Good evening," he addressed the pretty young blonde. "We're here for the New Year's Eve event."

"Welcome," she exclaimed. "What are your names?" Troy gave the information and they were waved into the main bar. "The event is this way. Sonya will show you to your table. Happy New Year!"

They followed her through the festively decorated bar area. Black, silver, and gold balloons floated along the ceiling, filling the room with glitzy ribbons that dangled within reach. They arrived at a narrow table with floor to ceiling windows framing the city below. Parker and Cameron were already there and stood to greet them as Troy vanished behind the scenes.

Parker's smile was joyous as he pulled Jenna in for a long hug. "You look so beautiful," he said.

She pulled back and admired his navy suit. "You look good yourself."

Cameron let out a quiet whistle as he pulled Veronica close. He wore a black suit with a black shirt beneath. "You look good enough to eat," he whispered near her ear.

His comment should have turned her on, but instead she bristled. "Nice suit," she replied as she pulled back.

"Check out our view," Cameron said as he pointed through the glass. They could see the entire city. Bridges glowed against the murky Willamette River and cars scurried along the many roads and twisted highway. The convention center and concert hall glowed as their strobe lights scanned the dark sky.

"I love this city," Jenna commented.

Parker busied himself by pouring champagne and made a joke, "I know this is a daring move, but I think I can manage this time, since it's already been uncorked."

Veronica shot him a look, then smirked as he handed the glasses around. He cleared his throat and said, "Here's to the happiest New Year yet."

They tapped glasses and in unison said, "Cheers."

Sitting next to Jenna on the burgundy leather sofa, Parker whispered, "I've missed you."

His words tickled her ear and brought a thrill along her spine. "I missed you too."

His mouth covered hers in a sweet kiss that she didn't want to end.

Cameron put his arm around Veronica. "How have you been the past couple of weeks?"

"It's been nice to be on winter break. What about you?"

"I've been busy wrapping up some year-end stuff with the accountant and preparing next year's budget. I've been thinking about you."

She took a sip of her bubbles and pressed, "Oh?"

"Yeah, I can't wait for this to be over so we can get on with it."

His dark eyes implored and she felt conflicted. Was she letting the past cloud her feelings or was it Troy's letter about puzzle pieces? She had to shake that off. Troy had no right to be so forward. She'd wanted to reunite with Cameron for years and now the chance was within reach. "That's sweet of you to say."

He leaned in and whispered, "You are seriously sexy tonight. I wish we could sneak away."

His familiarity should have been a comfort but it made her edgy, not knowing if Troy was still in the vicinity. The cloud of his interest was over her and she knew she had to put it aside. "Let's dance," she said and took his hand.

"It's a little early, but okay," he agreed and followed her to the dance floor.

Parker and Jenna barely noticed them leave, they were so deep in conversation. "How was Christmas with your family?" he asked.

Jenna smiled into his eyes. "It was fun. Veronica and her aunts joined us this year, which made it even better. I thought of you."

He kissed her cheek. "I thought about you too. It would have been fun to spend the day together."

Jenna felt warm and sated as she sat beside Parker. His words paired with the bubbly eased her deeper into his arms. She didn't dare jump ahead to "next year," but her mind did. "Do you want to dance?" she asked.

Parker's eyes sparkled. "I thought you'd never ask."

He stood and took her hand, leading her to the dance floor.

A DJ was set up in the corner busily clicking away at his laptop. His song selection was varied between top 40 hits and flashback music from the '50s to '80s. The dim lighting highlighted the city below as the growing crowd moved in time. Cameron and Veronica were dancing closely to the remake, "Show Me Love," by Sam Feldt and Kimberly Anne. The lyrics were telling and so was their body language.

Parker and Jenna approached, and Cameron gave a nod. Veronica's eyes held Jenna's for an instant until Parker took Jenna's hand and gave her a twirl. It was an unexpected thrill and she couldn't contain her smile as he pulled her near.

"Our first dance," he whispered in her ear.

A soft giggle escaped her and she replied, "Who knew you had such moves?"

"I blame my cousins. Whenever we all got together, the girls insisted on dance parties. There's nothing like a big family to get you past the awkwardness of dancing."

"You'll have to thank them for me."

"Maybe you can do it yourself sometime."

Parker's words had her quivering. Jenna's voice was husky as she replied, "Maybe I'd like that."

His kiss was painfully sweet and Jenna was lost in him. The job was a factor but it was becoming less important by the second. She'd never known anyone like him. He was capable, sweet, and kind. Parker was the person she'd always hoped to find and aside from their workplace challenge, he seemed flawless.

The DJ changed the vibe when he grabbed the mic. "How's everybody doing tonight?"

The crowd cheered.

"Are you ready to ring in the new year?"

More hoots rose from the crowd.

"Let's turn things up," he said and played "1999" by Prince.

The dance floor filled with more bodies excitedly grooving to the ever-popular tune. One couple stumbled into Parker and quickly righted themselves. They appeared to be in a drunken trance as they ground hips to the beat.

Cameron gave Veronica a spin and her dress lifted into a bell with the action. He whistled as she spun back to face him. "Your legs are scandalous, V."

He was as handsome as ever. His straight white teeth gleamed and his smile was contagious. She couldn't help but melt the past into the present. Her Cameron was back. His penetrating stare could liquify a glacier and she was no iceberg. His kiss was deep and unabashed. She let it happen, feeling the familiar demand of his needy tongue and his strong arms around her. They came up for air and he twirled her again. She was dizzy from it all. The tension she'd felt earlier after Troy picked them up, her questions about Cameron, and the turning action collided as she had a silent talk with herself. Tonight was about the present and future.

Jenna gave her shoulder a tap as they left the dance floor and went back to the table. Cameron asked, "Want to join them?"

"Sure," he agreed, "I could use a drink."

They arrived at the table to find Parker and Jenna with their noses practically pressed against the glass as they studied the skyline. "Can you believe we helped build that?" Jenna said in amazement.

"We have the best job." Parker replied.

Their eyes met and for the first time all night, the air

between them was uncomfortable. Veronica made their presence known. "Who's up for shots?"

Jenna and Parker turned and Cameron raised his hand like a child in class. "I am," he said with a cheeky smile.

A well-timed server arrived at their table. Cameron looked at the group, "What will it be, guys?"

Veronica spoke up, "We started the night with tequila."

"Tequila and champagne," Jenna said, "can't wait for tomorrow."

Cameron placed the order, "Four shots of Patron, please."

The server smiled and announced, "I'll be right back."

"Should we order some snacks to go with our booze?" Parker asked.

"Sure," Veronica said while picking up the menu. "Umm, how about egg rolls, chicken skewers and crab-stuffed wontons?"

"Yum," Jenna, agreed.

"Sounds good to me," Parker confirmed.

Moments later their smiling server returned with a tray of tiny glasses filled with clear liquid. "Here you are," she said as she handed them around. "Do you need anything else at the moment?"

Cameron gave her the order and returned his attention to the table. Raising his hand in a toast he said, "Here's to new beginnings!"

Their glasses clinked and they swallowed the alcohol as Ryan and Lanie arrived at their table.

"Good evening, everyone," Ryan greeted.

"Wow," Jenna exclaimed, "it's nice to see you both."

Veronica's fascination with Lanie's mound of a belly straining against the snug glittery blue dress was apparent. Lanie said, "Hi, Veronica. Do you want to touch it? He or she is kicking up a storm."

Veronica looked embarrassed and apologized. "I'm sorry. I didn't mean to stare."

Lanie laughed easily. "Don't be. It happens all the time. You wouldn't believe how often strangers gawk and ask to touch my stomach. At least you, I know. Go ahead," she encouraged.

Veronica tentatively placed her hand on Lanie's stomach in time to have it nearly kicked off by the child inside. "Oh my, that's strong. Does it make you nervous?"

Her expression was anything but scared. "Not anymore. When it first started happening, I worried all the time. Now, I'm more concerned about how the activity seems to peak late at night. I have a feeling there won't be much sleep when this," she placed a hand on her moving stomach, "little one arrives."

"Do you know the sex yet?" Jenna asked.

Lanie looked into Ryan's dark blue eyes and grinned. He answered for the both of them, "We're waiting until he or she is born."

"Aww," Veronica couldn't contain herself, "that's so sweet. I bet the suspense is killing you. Do you have a feeling?"

Lanie looked at Ryan and back at Veronica. "I kind of think it's a boy."

Ryan chimed, "And I think it's a girl."

The group chuckled, the men uneasily.

"Enough about us," Ryan said. "How are you guys doing this evening? This is your last date before the grand finale."

The table went quiet for an instant until the server arrived with their food. "It looks like your group is growing," she said.

"Can I get you two something to drink?"

Ryan looked at Lanie, "Can you make me something

festive and virgin?" Her head quirked toward her unmissable stomach.

"What about a Vellini, a virgin Bellini?"

Lanie agreed, "That sounds good."

"And for you?" She directed her attention to Ryan, taking a moment to admire his chiseled features.

"I'll have an IPA, thanks,"

"I'll be back," she announced as she retreated.

"Please," Parker waved his hand, "sit down."

Lanie and Ryan snugged at one side of a sofa as the others settled in.

"I haven't been here in a while," Lanie commented. "I see it's still the place to be," she said while surveying the mayhem. The dance floor was teeming with people dirty dancing to "Let's Get It On." Meanwhile, the bar was alive with men in pairs or groups hovering over tables filled with single women looking their best. There wasn't an empty chair in the place.

Cameron agreed, "Yes, it is."

Ryan noticed his tone and decided to ask, "How has your evening together been so far, Veronica?"

She swallowed her champagne hard and cleared her throat. "We haven't been here too long but we've already danced a few songs."

Her factual account gave him nothing while confirming his suspicions. From what he could tell, things weren't clicking between Cameron and Veronica this time around. "What do you think of the place, Jenna?"

She and Parker were holding hands and sitting quite close. "It's not something I'd normally do, which makes it all the more fun." Her eyes met Parker's and he smiled like an excited boy.

The server returned with their drinks. "Here you are." She placed a fizzing flute in front of Lanie and handed the beer to Ryan. "Do you need anything else at the moment?"

"No, thank you," Parker replied after surveying the table.

She left them as the DJ announced, "We're going to slow it down now. This song is for all the lovers." He tapped a button and "Can't Help Falling in Love," by Elvis Presley filled the room.

"Shall we, Mrs. Glass?" Ryan stood and took Lanie's hand.

She smiled like a woman in love as pushed herself off of the sofa. "I thought you'd never ask, Mr. Glass."

Jenna and Veronica let out a collective sigh as they watched them leave.

"Let's go, Jenna," Parker stood and pulled her to standing, leaving only Veronica and Cameron.

"Want to?" Cameron asked.

Veronica hesitated. "Let's sit this one out. It'll give us a few minutes to talk."

"Sure," Cameron said and took a drink. "Can we talk about breaking all the rules and spending the night together?"

Veronica studied Cameron's face. A few delicate lines formed at the corners of his dark eyes. His lips were as appealing as ever, but something was different now. Was it her? "Why would you want to do that?"

His eyebrows rose, "Spend the night with you? Are you mad? Why wouldn't I?" He nuzzled her ear, "You're amazing."

"What amazes you about me?"

Cameron shook his head, "I don't understand. Is this a test within the test?"

Veronica's sharp inhale was all the answer he would get.

"V, what's wrong? I thought we had a great time together in Bend."

After a pause, she replied, "It was fun."

"Fun?" he asked.

"Yes.

"Veronica, I didn't sign up for Love Test and follow through with the dates for fun."

"Why did you sign up?"

"I told you, I wanted to meet someone special. I was floored when we were matched. Are you unsure?"

Veronica felt like she was losing it. She'd wanted this for so long and now that he was here, she was circling mentally, trying to find a concrete reason why they should be together. "No, not doubts, but I want *us* to be sure. Our history shouldn't be the reason we end up together."

"V, we were good together back then and we still are. Life got in the way." He took their flutes from the table and handed Veronica hers. "Here's to a new year and a new beginning for us." He tapped his glass to hers and they drank. Their eyes locked and his lips found their home.

She kissed him too, receiving and giving the tenderness he felt for her. That was the moment when she set her annoying doubts down, Troy included. She decided to give Cameron the chance he deserved. "Let's get out of here, V. I want to be alone with you."

She knew they shouldn't leave, but she found herself wanting the intimacy of sex, as if it would seal their fate. He pulled her to standing as Ryan and Lanie returned to the table.

"Are you guys going to dance?" Lanie asked.

Cameron cleared his throat and Veronica agreed abruptly, "Caught us. We'll see you in a few."

"Have fun," Lanie called as they walked away.

Ryan's hand rested on Lanie's low back, "Sit for a minute."

Placing a hand on the arm of the couch, she eased onto the low sofa with a sarcastic chuckle, "I am so fat."

Rubbing her shoulders from behind, Ryan admonished, "Stop that. You're almost eight months pregnant and you look better than every woman here."

She shook her head. "Thank you but I feel like a blob."

"You're the prettiest blob in the room."

He sat beside her and rubbed her neck. "Have you been thinking about the house?"

She chuckled deeply, "It's been one of my obsessions today."

"You haven't mentioned it much."

"I know. I guess I don't want to get my hopes up. We've already been so fortunate, but sometimes luck runs out."

"What are you talking about, Lanie?"

"Nobody is this happy. I don't want to wish for anything more than what we already have."

"Lanie, it's a house, not luck. If we want it, all we have to do is buy it."

"Do you really think it will happen? We have a lot to do in selling our places."

"You are a woman who has earned every dream she's ever had and that house is no different. If it's what you want, we'll make it happen, together."

"What about you? Did you like the house as much as I did?"

Ryan killed her with his clear eyes and sly smirk. "I did and I promise, it'll be our home."

"If you keep looking at me that way, we won't make it until midnight."

"Who says we have to?"

"Mr. Glass, are you suggesting?"

"No, no, no, you don't get to blame me. You're the aggressor this time."

Lanie knew he was right and that she would spend the rest of her days seducing the man who wasn't supposed to be here. She rasped, "Ryan, take me home."

He cleared his throat and helped her up. On the way out, they waved a goodbye to the couples and hastily rushed for the elevator.

"Listen up, everyone," the DJ's voice boomed through the speakers, "gather around the dance floor," he waved his hands. "It's time for the countdown. Let's ring in this New Year."

The television behind him was tuned to Times Square and they looked on as the screen flashed the numbers starting with, "10." Jenna and Parker smiled into each other's eyes. "9," Veronica and Cameron clasped hands. "8, 7, 6, 5," the combined voices of the room shook the walls. "4, 3, 2, 1…"

"Happy New Year!" shouted the DJ as sparkles of confetti dropped from the ceiling and floated all around.

Parker pulled Jenna in for a kiss. His mouth said everything she was thinking, but he had to tell her. When he pulled back, he rested his forehead against hers and said, "I'm falling in love with you, Jenna."

Her throat caught, but she managed a reply, "I'm falling in love with you, too."

Cameron and Veronica held each other close and their tongues spoke volumes. Desire and history bonded them to the present. Her head spun from a combination of alcohol, nerves, and the unbelievable luck that rejoined them. Their kiss was interrupted by Parker's slap on Cameron's back. Veronica and Jenna hugged each other and the guys did the same.

"Hey," Veronica noted Jenna's glowing handbag, "your phone."

Jenna reached inside her purse and removed her phone. There was a message from her boss: "I wanted to start your New Year off in the best way. Congratulations, the promotion is yours."

Jenna's expression was crestfallen. Although she'd spent the past several years working toward this, the promotion would make her Parker's boss.

Parker noticed her expression. "What's the matter?"

"Can we talk?" she asked and led him toward the table.

Cameron's jacket pocket lit and he felt the vibration along with Veronica's attention. Unconcerned, he removed the phone from his pocket and Kyra's name flashed across the screen. Veronica's pulse raced as he ignored her call. It was as if time stood still. All sound ceased and even the confetti seemed to move in slow motion. A bell announced her message. Cameron was about to put the phone away, but Veronica wasn't having it. "What does it say?"

His color disappeared as he tapped the voice mail icon and read the transcript, "Happy New Year, Cammy. I hope you get everything you wish for this year."

Veronica couldn't hold her emotions at bay any longer. The nagging doubts that clouded this process weren't just her insecurities. Cameron and Kyra were still connected and the proof was right in front of her. She wouldn't wait for him anymore. "I'm leaving and I don't want you to follow me," she spat, "Cammy."

She turned on her heel and bolted for the elevator. Fortunately, the doors were open so she hurried inside and hit the door close button. She felt ill and like she may faint. Leaning against the ornate wood walls of the cab, she was reduced to tears. The elevator bell rang, announcing her arrival at the lobby. Wiping her face with the back of her hands, she straightened her shoulders and strode out the doors.

Troy was perched on a leather chair. He stood to greet her. Searching her face, he could see the pain. Without a word, he followed her through the door and pointed toward the parked car.

She was silent on the drive back to her place. An emptiness consumed her spirits even as dry tears itched her cheeks. Whatever had been between her and Cameron, she knew tonight would erase it all. No matter his explanation, she wouldn't be comfortable with him again. It was something she'd grappled with since they were reunited and she could no longer convince herself otherwise.

They arrived at her house and she didn't wait for Troy to open the door. He stood helplessly on the sidewalk as she grappled with the keys and made her way inside.

CAMERON HOPED VERONICA WOULD RETURN. He furiously texted her to come back, telling her that he and Kyra were only friends. He approached the table where Parker and Jenna stood, hoping she'd be there so he could explain.

Parker and Jenna looked anything but happy as he arrived. "Hey," he said.

"Hey, yourself," Parker replied.

"Where's V?" Jenna's question was more of a demand.

"Well, she's a little upset."

"Why?" Jenna barked.

"My ex. She called and Veronica lost it."

"Oh, no," Parker replied, "I thought you only spoke once in a while."

Jenna gasped. "What? You knew they were still in touch and you didn't tell me?"

Parker ran his hand through his hair and tried to explain, "It wasn't my place, Jenna."

She closed her eyes and shook her head. "Maybe we've both forgotten our place. I'm going to find Veronica."

Parker reached for Jenna's arm. "Let me help you."

Her expression was as murky as their work situation as she said, "It's best I do this alone."

———

WITH HIS DEADLINE LOOMING, Ryan decided to interview Cameron and Parker over the phone. The phone rang and on the third ring, Cameron picked up. "Hello."

"Hi, Cameron. It's Ryan. How are you today?"

His voice was rough as he replied, "I'm okay. How are you, Ryan?"

"Good, thanks. Should we get started?"

"Sure, sure," he replied.

"Well, we're nearing the end and rather than ask you a bunch of questions, I've only one: What do you want to happen between you and Veronica?"

Cameron let out a sarcastic chuckle. "I'm not sure it matters what I want. I think Veronica's mind is made up—probably always was—and I lost out. I let her go years ago and she's never forgiven me."

Ryan was no therapist and he disliked the fact that he was in the midst of this dating challenge, but he had a job to do. "Should she forgive you?"

The silence was awkward but Ryan waited. Finally, Cameron replied, "I don't know. Maybe not. Do you have anything else to ask?"

"Will you be at the decision date?"

Cameron let out a snort. "I need get back to you about that."

"Cameron, are you okay?"

"I'm fine," he said. "Take care, Ryan," and the line went dead.

Ryan didn't know what had happened, but he was certain that whatever it was, Cameron wasn't happy about it.

He tried to shake the nagging emotions of Cameron as he dialed Parker's number. "Hello," Parker's voice came through.

"Hey, Parker. It's Ryan. How are you today?"

"Ugh, I'm okay. How are you?"

"Doing fine, thanks for asking."

"Sure."

"Well, I won't keep you long, but you know the drill."

"Yep," Parker replied.

"I've planned only one question. What do you want to happen between you and Jenna after the event is over?"

Parker cleared his throat and said, "All I want is Jenna, but it's not only up to me."

Ryan's plan of asking only one questions was pointless. "What do you think Jenna wants?"

"I, I don't know. She's pretty pissed at me and we have a work situation to contend with."

"Is she angry about work?"

"No. Well, I don't think so. If anyone should be angry about that it would be me. After all, I tried to talk to her about it and she wanted to hold off. She's the one who got the job and I could care less. I love her."

Ryan's eyes grew wide but he kept his tone even. "You love her?"

Parker was silent. "Yes, but it may not matter. I fucked up and she probably won't forgive me."

"Wait a minute. What happened?"

Parker explained, "I knew Cameron was still in touch with his ex, the one he left Veronica for, and I didn't tell Jenna."

"Yikes. How did you know?"

"She texted him when we were in Bend and I happened to see. We talked about it and he made it seem like they were just friends, but I had a feeling it was more than that. I guess I should have told Jenna, but I didn't know if it was my place to meddle."

"I can understand that. You were in a tough spot. Jenna must understand."

"I don't know. She was furious when she found out and we haven't spoken since. Also, she got the promotion and I'm sure that's making her second guess our relationship."

Ryan was perplexed. He thought Parker and Jenna were a sure thing. They seemed in sync and from all he could tell, though he was no expert, they seemed to have what it took. "Have you told her you love her?"

"I...kind of," he replied.

"Kind of doesn't cut it, Parker. If you love her, she needs to know. You've already held back by not letting her know about Cameron's connection with his ex. Don't hold this back too."

"But the job. She's worked so hard for it. How can I cause problems for her?"

Ryan chuckled, "Maybe I should remind you how Lanie and I got together. If you love her, cause a problem so big that she can't say no."

8

BREAKING THE RULES

The morning-after hangover wasn't the only painful reality that crushed Jenna as she stirred in her bed. When the night began, all she could think about was seeing Parker again. Her worries about their work situation weren't just on the back burner, they weren't even on the range, but the night turned on her and instead of waking up to Parker's dreamy eyes, hers were stinging and swollen from sobbing herself to sleep.

If Jenna had learned anything from being a project manager, it was that problems don't go away, especially when they aren't dealt with. They bubble up again when you've nearly forgotten they exist, rising at the worst possible moment and reminding you of what you tried to gloss over. Her head ached as she pulled the blankets off and sat at the edge of the bed. She headed to the kitchen to start the coffee as her brain rattled around in agony.

"Hey," Veronica called from the kitchen doorway. Her mascara was smeared and she wore her favorite old robe. It was tattered at the edges and the softness had worn away. Although Jenna had gotten her a new one for Christmas,

Veronica preferred the comfort of the one she'd had since she was a teenager.

"Morning," Jenna replied without a smile.

Jenna pulled two mugs from the cupboard and the milk from the refrigerator. Filling the automatic frother with milk, she turned to her friend and asked, "How are you doing?"

Veronica's eyes pooled but she swiftly blinked the threatening tears away. Her defiance was short lived as she failed to keep her emotions contained and began crying like a child. Jenna felt no stronger, but she tried to be for Veronica. She hugged her friend and together they resorted to tears.

Finally, Jenna said, "Let's sit."

Veronica ambled to the dining table and dropped into a plush chair. Jenna went for the coffee maker and poured their cups. "Here," she said as she placed a café au lait in front of her best friend.

"Thanks," Veronica managed while wiping her face with her robe.

Jenna took a seat and huffed. "So much for the start of this year. I had hoped Parker and I would end up breaking the rules to spend last night together. Instead, I'm not sure if we'll even continue what we started."

Veronica studied her friend. Her large eyes were puffy and her hair was wound into a messy pile on top of her head. "I know you're crazy about him. How would you like to see the work situation play out? Maybe there is still a way."

Jenna contemplated her coffee mug as she said, "And what about the fact that he knew Kyra and Cameron were still in touch? He didn't tell me. I don't like secrets."

Despite her deflated mood, Veronica managed to find a bit of fight as she set Jenna straight. "You would have done the exact same thing if the situation were reversed. It wasn't his place to tell us. It was Cameron's. Don't blame Parker for that."

Jenna knew she was right. She'd already considered it from that vantage point and she knew she'd do the same. It also struck her that Parker tried to discuss the work scenario and she was the one to brush it off. Things were going so well that she didn't want to face the inevitable. It was as much her fault, if not more, that they hadn't put a plan together, assuming they wanted to continue the relationship. What if Parker didn't want to keep seeing her? That didn't seem likely—he was the one who had tried to discuss the situation.

Veronica said, "Your mind is racing. What are you thinking?"

Jenna shook her head in dismay, "I'm not thinking clearly and I haven't been since the night we were paired. What about you? I mean after five years, Cameron returns and not just returns, but he's proven to be your ideal mate, and then the person who put a wedge between you those years ago comes back too. It's like history is repeating itself. What are you going to do?"

A cocktail of fury and humiliation propelled Veronica's statement. "There's nothing to do. Cameron isn't mine. He has proven that twice. Instead of holding on to what could have been, I need to face what actually is. Six years and two breakups later and they're still in touch. It's not over for them, but it is over for he and I."

Jenna didn't disagree but she also knew that Veronica could be intimidating. Maybe that was what kept Cameron from telling her he was friends with Kyra. "Do you really think he signed up for the Love Test while still in love with Kyra?"

Veronica shook her head. "I don't know. That part is confusing."

"Could it be that they really are only friends, but he didn't tell you for obvious reasons? I'm sure he knew how upset you'd be and that you wouldn't even give him a chance if you knew."

The torch of hope that Veronica once carried for her relationship with Cameron flickered briefly. "Do you think it's my fault?"

"No, absolutely not!" Jenna went on, "He should have told you from the beginning but after my reluctance to discuss the work situation with Parker, I can understand his procrastinating, especially as things were just getting started, or in your case, restarted."

Veronica swirled the coffee in her mug in silence. "What are we going to do?"

Jenna shook her head in silence.

━━━

THE FIRST OF the year was always quiet at the gallery, which Lanie and Jay took full advantage of. It was the perfect time to rearrange the displays without disturbing patrons. Lanie stood back as Jay hung a wall sculpture. "A little to the right," she directed.

He moved the piece slightly.

"A little more," she said as the door chimed, announcing a visitor.

Lanie peeked toward the entrance and found Audrey carrying a box of Voodoo Doughnuts. "This is a surprise."

Audrey smiled like a child. "I was craving doughnuts and I knew you'd be my partner in crime."

The sickly-sweet aroma of maple syrup permeated the

air between them as Audrey greeted her friend. They hugged and Lanie snatched the box from her.

"Hope you brought enough to share," Jay complained as he got down from the ladder.

Audrey hissed, "You know I did."

Lanie tossed open the lid and studied the options inside. "Smart—you got three bacon maple bars and my favorite, sprinkles!"

"Yes, I know what you and this little monster," she touched Lanie's stomach, "like."

"Want some coffee?" Lanie asked.

"Um, I think I've had my fill for today. Thanks though."

Jay came to hover over the box and quickly snatched a maple-glazed donut that was topped with two pieces of bacon. "Mmm, these are definitely made with crack."

"I'm sure," said Audrey as she took a bite of one covered in powdered sugar.

"Let's sit," Jay demanded as he confiscated the box and brought it to the table. The ladies followed the box and sat across from one another as Jay rooted around in the refrigerator.

He came back with a pitcher and three metal cups. "Here," he said as he filled Audrey's cup first, "drink this. It's my special blend."

Audrey took a sip of the colorful concoction. It was creamy and tasted of orange and ginger with a spicy zing that lingered. "Interesting. What is it?"

"This is Lanie's health elixir," he said while sitting on the bench beside Lanie. "Well, anyone can use it but I make it especially for her."

Audrey's eyes grew wide and fixated on Lanie who stifled a laugh. "Yes, Jay you've been remarkable with the recipes and in helping me exist without coffee."

"What's in it?" Audrey questioned but didn't stop drinking.

"Juices, oat milk, herbs, a few spices, all good things."

"You're being vague." Audrey called an audible and peered at Lanie. "He's being vague. Right?"

She nodded. "A little, but it's his proprietary blend. I don't need the recipe as long as he keeps making it."

"I see you finally learned how to delegate," she chided.

Jay mumbled, "I don't know about that."

Lanie gave him a playful shove.

"Be careful. You don't want to hurt yourself or that little alien inside of you."

"Shut up. You're the alien," Lanie lobbed like a child.

He chuckled and took a bite of his donut. With his mouth still full he managed, "Can I ask you guys something?"

The women looked at one another then Jay. "Sure."

"Do you think something is wrong with me?"

Their expressions of surprise matched as they asked over one another, "Why do you ask?"

Jay couldn't even laugh at their jinx. "Serge asked me to marry him again—actually, for the third time—and I still can't say yes."

"What?" Audrey was freaking out. "Wait, three times? When did this happen?"

Jay rolled his eyes and said, "The first time was after Halloween, but I attributed that to our acid trip, so I blew it off. Next, he asked me on Christmas morning over mimosas. He used the foil from the champagne bottle as a faux ring. It was cute, but I didn't think he was serious and I said as much. Next, he asked me after our midnight kiss on New Year's Eve…" His gaze went distant.

The ladies wanted details. Audrey wouldn't hold back. "What was there left to say by the third time around?"

Jay's eyes misted. To pull himself together, he jutted his chin and blinked away the tears. "He said that he knew from the start I was the one for him. He said he knows he's never going to be the love of my life, but if I marry him," his chin quivered, "he'll make sure that I love the rest of my life."

Lanie's mouth dropped open and even Audrey was stunned into silence. When she finally found her voice, she said the most unexpected thing: "Why does he want to get married?"

Jay looked perturbed, "Why, well...umm, why wouldn't he want to marry me?"

Audrey shook her head. "No, I get that, but does he? Is that what you're worried about? Does he know you well enough for the commitment? Do you know him? What will married life be like? Does he want kids? Do you? I mean, there are so many unanswered questions. No wonder you're hesitant."

Jay's eyes were bugging out of his head now. He asked, "How much caffeine have you had today?"

Jay turned to Audrey's question in earnest. "It's true, some of that has crossed my mind, but mostly, I don't want to fuck up and I don't trust myself to make a lifetime commitment. I love Serge and hurting him would be unbearable. If we get married, I probably will."

Lanie knew she wasn't one to talk on the subject of marriage since her first engagement had ended in her marrying another man, but she had to set Jay straight on one thing. "What you're saying makes sense except you've been doing a pretty good job of keeping it," she raised a brow, "in your pants for over a year now. You don't even check other guys out anymore or for that matter, notice when they're into you. I think you're ready and Serge is the one."

Jay's expression remained bleak as he replied, "I notice, I just pretend I don't."

"That sounds like a man ready for marriage to me," Audrey exclaimed. "We all notice and we all pretend we don't, because we know that what we have is worth more."

"Well, not everyone only looks. Trust me on this and it's not only fidelity that concerns me. What if we stop vibing and we get to be an old, grouchy couple eating silently at a restaurant?"

Lanie started laughing now. "You need to come down off the ledge, friend. Most couples become grouchy when they're old and they don't care about making small talk anymore. I don't know about vibing, but wouldn't it be nice to have someone to grow old with?"

Audrey teased, "Boy this conversation is like de ja vu. I'm pretty sure I played Lanie the first time around."

Jay looked wistful and glanced through the window unseeing. "I'd planned to grow old with Sebastian; look how that turned out."

Lanie touched Jay's arm. "I'm sorry, Jay. I know you still miss him, but it's not a betrayal to him if you marry Serge. I'm sure he would want you to be happy."

Jay pursed his lips and managed a snarky reply. "I don't know about that. He was a little jealous. I kind of liked it about him."

Audrey laughed, "That's it—you're twisted and Serge isn't the drama type so it's throwing you."

"No," Jay defended. "Serge is the drama type which is why he keeps asking a person who doesn't believe in marriage to marry him."

Audrey shook her head. "Serge is a good guy. I hope things will be okay between you."

Jay's retort was pissy. "Of course they will. We're not breaking up. I just didn't agree to marry him." He stood from the table and turned on his heel. "I remembered I have an errand to run. Thanks for the donuts, Aud. I'll be back shortly."

They watched his rushed escape and when the door shut, Audrey turned to Lanie. "How are *you* feeling?"

Her hand moved automatically to her belly. "Mostly great, sometimes tired. With our houses about to be on the market and our lives in limbo, I'm not in the spot I'd imagined I'd be for my first child's arrival."

Audrey leaned forward. "When will you know about," she put on a snooty tone, "the palace at the park?"

Lanie sniffed, "Tomorrow, the realtor said. We'll know by tomorrow."

"And when will your places be posted for sale?"

Lanie bit her lower lip, "This afternoon."

"Then there's nothing left to do but eat doughnuts, right?"

Lanie pushed the lid of the box open and plucked a pink and sprinkled ring from inside, "You're exactly right."

———

JENNA TOOK the stairs to the sixth floor arriving at the office by 6:30 a.m. on Monday morning. Only the whir of copy machines disturbed the silence. Lights automatically switched on as she walked down the corridor and into her small, glass-walled office.

She set her bag down on the chair and slid out her laptop. As she turned to dock it, she saw an envelope with her name scrawled across the front. With shaky fingers, she picked up the envelope and ran her thumb over her name.

Jenna hung her bag absently and sunk into her chair. The letter opener on her desk was a beacon. It gleamed under the lamp, silently egging her on. If she didn't open it, she'd be distracted, scratch that, even more distracted all day. One resolute swipe with the blade and the answers unfolded.

JENNA,

The first time I saw you, we were in a staff meeting and you were giving a project update. I'll never forget how you commanded the room. You were a stranger to me and I felt proud of you. From that day on, I've wanted to get to know you, outside of work.

If it weren't for us matching on Love Test, I wouldn't have asked you out and for the reasons we both know. But—we did match and we agreed to see it through. I meant everything I said to you and I know there's a way.

Be my Valentine?

Parker

P.S.—Sorry I didn't tell you about Cameron's old girlfriend texting him. I wasn't sure how to handle that. Hope Veronica is okay.

P.P.S.—Also, I know this note breaks the rules, but some rules are meant to be broken.

JENNA SAT BACK in her chair and briefly closed her weary eyes. When she opened them, she took the letter and placed it in the bottom drawer of her desk. She had five weeks before the final Love Test date she'd agreed to. For now, a cup of coffee was in order.

VERONICA STOOD beside Timothy's desk, watching as he worked out the problem: $601 + 130 =$

He quickly jotted the 1 to the right, a 3 in the center

and finally the 7 to start. "Excellent, Timmy. You're getting the hang of this."

The door opened and a student aide cleared her throat. Veronica looked up and in her arms was a crystal vase containing lavender roses with sprigs of lavender spaced in between. "Thank you," she stammered. "On the desk, please."

The mousy fourth grader nodded and left the flowers before scurrying out of the room. The clock struck 11:50 a.m. and the bell rang, announcing that it was time for break. "Be back on time, everyone, and for those of you who brought, don't forget your lunches."

When the last student rushed out, Veronica was left to face the gloriously frightening arrangement and her hopeful heart that wished for things she'd dared not believe in. With her inner conflict heightened, she nervously removed the tiny envelope that was perched in the center of the bouquet. The card inside had a cartoon image of a man crawling out of a dog house, confirming instantly who had sent them. She pushed past her irrational disappointment and read the sentiment:

V,

I'm sorry I messed up again. I handled it though. I won't talk to her anymore. I swear, we were just friends. Please give me another chance, please.

Love,
Cameron

THE WORDS and his gesture of the flowers should have cheered her, but they didn't. Veronica felt heavy and perplexed. Thankfully, she had five weeks to think about it. She decided to have ice cream for lunch.

RYAN HELD the door for Erve as he ducked in out of the rain. The pub was dim and cast in an aura of vintage from the hundred-year-old rugs to the wooden booths and period windows. A fire burned at the center of the space. "Table for two?" asked the stout, salt and pepper haired man in a black apron.

"Yes," Erve replied.

"Anywhere you like," he waved his hand. "I'll bring menus."

Erve guided them to a table by the window and removed his coat before taking a seat. Ryan joined as the server set the menus down. "Do you want something to drink first?"

"Iced tea for me," Erve said.

"Two, please," Ryan agreed.

"Be right back," he said and turned.

They opened the menus and quickly scanned the options. Erve said, "I don't know why I always do this. They never change it and I never order anything different."

"That's true," Ryan said. "You should."

"Why? There's no need to experiment when there's no need to experiment."

Ryan had heard Erve say that every time they'd eaten at the restaurant. "Well, I am going to get something different. For once, I'm trying the Cobb."

Erve squawked, "A salad?"

"Yeah, I put on a few over the holidays and, you know, eating with Lanie."

Their server returned with the iced teas and asked, "What would you like for lunch?"

Erve spoke up, "I'll have the pastrami with kraut and macaroni salad on the side and the kid'll have the Cobb salad, hold the dressing."

Ryan shook his head and asked, "Can you please put the dressing on the side?"

"Thanks, guys," said the server with a smirk on his face, "I'll put it in."

"What's your name again?" asked Ryan.

"It's Nico."

"Thanks, Nico."

Erve picked up his iced tea and took a gulp, despite the cold weather and potential for brain freeze. "Ahh, gotta love that feeling. Wakes me up every time."

"You're such a kid, Erve."

"Speaking of..." he sipped again as Ryan waited, "you're about to have one."

Ryan took a swallow of his own, feeling the cold liquid speed down his throat. "In approximately five weeks," he said.

Erve leaned forward. "Are ya nervous?"

Ryan couldn't avoid his beady black-eyed stare. "A little."

"That's good. It's normal. What scares you the most?"

A range of emotions flashed across his face as if he were imagining a hundred different scenarios at once—which he was.

Erve fidgeted with his straw and said, "Let me guess: you're afraid of the delivery, wondering what your sex life will be like after and questioning if you'll know how to take care of the baby, will you be a good dad, how will your marriage and life change, and is it all worth it?"

Ryan stared stunned at his friend, and boss, who'd

summed the bulk of his concerns into one terribly put together, run-on sentence. He finally managed to ask, "And?"

Erve huffed, his mouth held a grim line until he finally said, "Life is one big experiment. No one has the answer to these questions."

Ryan replied sarcastically, "This from the guy who doesn't even vary his lunch order."

"Life is an experiment, but lunch doesn't have to be."

Ryan grumbled, "You're getting on my nerves today."

"Look, all I'm saying is you can't worry about what is coming. Focus on the moment, what you can control, and let the rest unfold. What's happening with the house situation?"

Ryan sat upright. "Both places are on the market and there has been a lot of activity. The realtor thinks we'll have offers soon. The owner of the new house is ready to close when we are, so it's in the works."

"You're going to miss your place and especially that slip."

Ryan shrugged. "I decided to sell the boat."

"What?" Erve's eyes grew wide, "Why? You love that thing!"

Ryan met Erve's gaze. "We needed some cash for the offer and I don't use the boat enough to justify the expense."

"That's very adult of you," Erve's bushy brows knit together. "Hopefully Lanie knows how much that gesture means."

"She doesn't know I sold it."

Erve practically shouted, "What?" Thankfully they were alone in the pub.

"It doesn't matter. I'd rather have the extra money in case we need it than a boat I use a few times a year because you're right, without the slip outside my door, I wouldn't have taken it out much."

"I understand your reasoning, but why not tell Lanie?"

"She wouldn't have let me do it. We had our first real date on that boat. I think the house is a lot more important, but she would have made a fuss."

"And you don't think she's going to make one when she finds out you sold it?"

Ryan was saved from having to respond when Nico returned with Erve's monster sandwich and his salad.

THEY WERE FINISHING up a dinner of pizza and salad when Lanie's phone rang. "It's the realtor," she said as she answered. Ryan looked on with interest.

"Hi, Isabell. Hold on, Ryan is here. Let me put you on speaker."

"Ryan, Lanie?" Isabell called, "Can you both hear me?"

"We can," Ryan answered.

"I have good news. Both properties have received full-price offers and Lanie's has two. I'm sending the details via email. Will you look them over and give me a call back?"

Lanie's belly flopped. As excited as she was about the new place, a pang of anxiety crept in as she thought about saying goodbye to the last vestige of her independence, her condo. To give herself a minute, she said, "I'll go get my laptop."

Ryan nodded, "I'll clear the dishes." As he filled the dishwasher, Ryan remembered his earlier conversation with Erve. He knew eventually he'd have to tell Lanie about the boat and wondered if tonight was the time.

"Hey," Lanie said as she placed the computer on the island, "what's with the faraway look?"

His eyes locked on to her as he approached. "I need to tell you something."

Ryan's tone had her worried. "What's wrong?"

He shook his head, "Nothing is wrong. It's just, I made a decision and I sold the boat."

Lanie's expression was confused, "You what?"

"When we decided to go for the house, I contacted a guy who has been interested in my boat for a while. He bought it."

"Why did you do that?"

"I wanted us to have money for the deposit and an extra cushion and I knew we didn't need the added expense of a slip and boat maintenance when we won't be using it often."

A cocktail of emotions welled in Lanie. Guilt, for her reluctance about selling her condo and for his selfless act. Also, she was upset that he didn't discuss it with her first. "You love that boat and it's where we had our first date."

"I love you more," he said while reaching for her tummy, "and this little person."

She wanted to be mad but instead she was embarrassed and overwhelmed. "You should have talked to me about it first. I had money saved for this."

"I know you do and so do I, but who knows what will come up. It's not just me anymore, or the two of us. Another person is coming and we have to be ready for anything."

For the first time since they'd met, Lanie saw Ryan was afraid. "You do know we can't be ready for *anything*. The fact that you and I are together is proof of that. Life is going to send us surprises, which we can handle as long as we're together."

"I know and I'm sorry I did it without consulting you. I want to be strong for you and for you to know I'll take care of us," he leaned close and rested his forehead against hers, "of all of us."

"That's very old fashioned and noble of you, but don't do it again. We're partners, even if things get uneven sometimes."

Ryan caressed her cheek and gingerly kissed her lips.

When they parted he asked, "Shall we examine our offers, Mrs. Glass?"

This time Lanie's stomach flopped in a good way. "I'm ready if you are, Mr. Glass."

9

A VALENTINE'S DAY RECKONING

Lanie awoke with a start and was momentarily confused by her surroundings. The smell of bacon wafted and the morning light streamed through the sheer panels at the window. Her hand went automatically toward her distended belly as she surveyed the boxes strewn around. They'd just moved into the new home yesterday. A smile curved her mouth and a fresh batch of tears brimmed as she let the joy of their great fortune wash over her. She'd dared to dream and found the man who fit so naturally it was effortless.

"Good morning, wife." His smooth voice tickled her ears as he entered the bedroom carrying a tray laden with pancakes, bacon, and gorgeous red and white striped roses. "Happy Valentine's Day."

She managed to sit as he placed the tray on the bed. "Happy Valentine's Day, husband."

He kissed her swollen lips and smiled mischievously as he tugged something from his back. "I know we agreed not to exchange gifts since we spent so much on the house and baby stuff, but I saw this and couldn't resist." He shook a container of whipped cream and teased, "I hope you can't either."

Against nature, Lanie found herself wanting Ryan as much as ever. He was her aphrodisiac despite the fact that she was nine months along. She rasped, "You know me so well."

Their kiss tugged a mutual desire that neither could avoid since the first moment they met. Tongues teased and retreated in a dance that they'd perfected in their short marriage. Still, the boxes surrounded them, and today they'd agreed to a baby shower at the Mains' house before the Love Test finale this evening. She pulled back and demanded, "Okay, but it has to be a quickie. We have so much to do today."

Ryan's bass-filled chuckle was followed by a barb, "So demanding," he replied. "I'm happy to oblige."

He tugged his T-shirt off and dropped his flannel pajama bottoms. Lanie admired his toned mid-section with great fascination now that her stomach had become a giant watermelon. After pushing the tray to the far end of the bed, he teased her camisole overhead exposing her enormous breasts and tummy. It amazed him how much he wanted her, even more since she was carrying their child. "You are stunning."

A moment of insecurity crossed her face but he kissed it away. His tongue erased any doubts, as did his skillful hands. He caressed her breasts and she felt the heat rise. He pulled back and said, "Are you ready for your gift."

She purred, "Uh huh."

He shook the container and took aim with the nozzle. The cool cream felt decadent against her nipples and he covered both with ease. "Don't move," he demanded as she rested against the pillows. He lowered his face to her breasts and tapped his tongue through the cream, grazing each nipple and smiling like a child. She squirmed and he held her wrists. "Stay still."

Her laugh was muffled as the battering continued. A tap was followed by a lick and finally, he suckled, repeating the action on both sides. She writhed under his command. A contraction tightened her stomach as his assault continued. He cleared his throat and took the whipped cream in hand. His moves were torturous as he pulled the blankets down. "Lay back."

Lanie didn't always like to submit, but Ryan had a power over her that she couldn't deny. She edged herself lower, enjoying the power of being naughty. He opened her legs and with a fiendish expression aimed the cream at her spot. The shock of cold against her was indecently arousing. Ryan tossed the container aside and buried himself in the sticky froth. His tongue tormented her to the height of arousal until she tugged his hair. "Now, please."

He couldn't help himself as his knowing tongue lingered inside of her. She whimpered before he finally drew back. Cream rested beneath his nose. Lanie couldn't resist wiping it away then sucking her own finger. His erection was bursting as he devoured her mouth and moved her toward the edge of the bed. His eyes held a tenderness as he stood over her and entered her heavenly cave.

———

THEY ARRIVED AT THE MAINS' house ten minutes late after their morning in bed and Lanie's insistence that she unpack some of the boxes before leaving. As happy as she was to have found their new home, she wished they could have been settled before the baby arrived. With the frequent Braxton Hicks contractions she was experiencing today, she wondered if they'd have the time.

The door burst open as the pack of dogs and Mr. and Mrs. Main greeted them. "Lanie," Annette Main cooed, "you look ethereal."

Lanie shook her head as they embraced. "I look like a whale."

"All women feel that way when they're pregnant," she admonished. "Let me have your coats."

Ryan shook Thomas Main's hand in greeting. "Thank you for hosting us."

"Nonsense. We wouldn't have it any other way." The old man's blue eyes twinkled. "Everyone is here and situated in the living room."

Ryan followed Thomas Main and Lanie walked beside Annette Main after she hung their coats. She wrapped her arm around Lanie's and they meandered toward the familiar sound of their closest friends.

Erve and his wife Anne were there, Jay and Serge stood side by side, Audrey and Ron doted on Lee and Lily, wringing their hands and fearful that the toddlers would break something at any moment. Lanie felt a profound sense of belonging as she soaked it all in.

The long dining table was laden with food. Smoked salmon surrounded cream cheese, roasted vegetables, salads, pasta, bread and an assortment of cheese covered every square inch. A pitcher of spiced apple cider rested at the center beside three tiers of intricately decorated, heart-shaped petit fours.

"This looks amazing," Lanie exclaimed. "You didn't have to go to such trouble."

"Please, I didn't do much. Audrey and Jay helped with everything."

Audrey came to stand near her friend, "Thank you, sister," Lanie said as they embraced. Once again, tears threatened to spill from Lanie's eyes.

"You don't need to thank me. I had a great time doing it. We," she gestured toward Jay, "had a great time doing it."

Jay took his turn at hugging his boss and friend. "How was your first night in the dream house?" he asked.

It was still a shock to her and she said as much, "When I woke up this morning, I forgot where I was. I can't believe it's ours."

"You deserve it, Lanie." Jay's eyes danced as he studied her. "And look at you. What woman looks like this when she's nine months pregnant?" He whistled and studied her cream smock dress. "I love the fabric."

The doorbell rang and Serge announced, "I'll get it."

A moment later Serge returned with four men all wearing matching beige suits and red ties. "I have a surprise for everyone. Please welcome the Fabulous Four. They're going to sing the barbershop quartet rendition of 'I Only Have Eyes for You.'"

The men lined up as one tapped his toe and counted in. Suddenly the room was filled by their practiced harmonies. High and low voices moved the group until even the babies were standing at attention. The tall ceilings and thick rugs absorbed their acapella tones and warmed them all. Ryan moved to beside Lanie as they watched the performance. Serge stood with Jay and as the song ended, the room burst with applause and hoots.

"Amazing!" cried Annette Main.

"You were all so good," announced Audrey.

Erve whistled.

Lanie cheered, "Thank you so much for arranging this, Serge."

He raised his hand and said, "I have something to say, if you'll indulge me."

The room went quiet. "The day I met you both," his

eyes shot from Jay to Lanie, "was one of the most impor-tant of my life. Meeting this man," he squeezed Jay's arm, "has changed everything. It wouldn't have happened if you didn't get him out of the gallery and into the restaurant. Chance is incredible, the way one minor event can alter the course of one's life. I'm forever grateful to you for bringing him to me and I wish you, Ryan, and the child we're here to celebrate," he placed a hand on Lanie's stom-ach, "a lifetime of joy."

"Hear, hear," Thomas Main agreed.

He faced Jay, taking his hand and in a move that surprised them all, got down on one knee. "My world came alive when you sat at my table. Knowing you is like finding another part of myself I didn't know was missing. You are the most exciting person I've ever known and I cannot imagine my life without you. Please, finally say you'll be mine. Marry me?"

The silence seemed eternal as Jay looked into Serge's pleading eyes and they all held their breath. Finally, Jay managed to speak. His voice was monotone. "You've made a spectacle here and put me on the spot." He paused dramatically, "It seems you know me well enough to realize I can't resist a public declaration. I never expected you, yet here you are, and it seems you're here to stay." He inhaled deeply, "So, yes. I will marry you."

The room roared with applause as everyone hugged and rejoiced in their engagement. The choir began their rendition of "Going to the Chapel."

When the song came to an end, Serge hugged and kissed his soon-to-be husband then made his way toward Ryan and Lanie. "I'm sorry to steal your thunder today, but I couldn't imagine a dreamier way to ask him. This is the fourth time!"

She hugged him and exclaimed, "Do not apologize.

This is the perfect way to celebrate our great prosperity. "We're happy for you both."

Mr. and Mrs. Main were arm and arm, Erve and Anne smiled joyously, and Audrey and Ron held their young with great smiles on their faces.

"This is so romantic," Audrey exclaimed. "I was going to wait, but it seems like this is the best time to tell everyone." She looked up at Ron, "Honey, I have a Valentine's Day surprise for you…"

Ron's eyes widened, "Oh?"

"I'm pregnant."

His smile lit up the room as he wrapped his free arm around Audrey, smashing the babies between them. "Our family is growing! Did you hear that, everyone?"

Ryan wrapped his arm around Lanie and in that moment all the troubles he'd seen and the sadness of the past vanished. For once, the images of disaster and war-torn countries, of losing his friend Madoc, were not to be recalled. Only happiness surrounded them as their lives combined into this incredible bond with the people who helped them find one another.

———

THEY RODE in the back of the limo in silence as an unfamiliar driver named Mark drove them to their final date before the decision. The women had made a pact not to talk about New Year's Eve or their thoughts until the final date was behind them. They knew they'd have to live with their own choices and they'd support each other, no matter what.

Veronica looked stunning in her long sleeved and fitted black dress, even if her expression didn't match. Her mind wandered from Cameron to Troy, whom she hadn't seen since New Year's Eve. A pang of disappointment came over her when Mark arrived to drive them. She reminded herself that the decision had nothing to do with Troy. It was about her and Cameron, the past, present, and—dare she imagine it—the future.

Jenna wore a knitted white skirt and matching top that fit her like a glove. Her brow furrowed as she thought of Parker and the promotion she'd accepted. Though she hadn't seen him since New Year's Eve, she wondered how they would work together when his project in Eastern Oregon ended. She recalled her Christmas gift to him— the book with the inscription about cooking together. For the first time since their first date, she felt trepidation going into the night.

They pulled to a stop at the Hotel Monaco and gave one another a contemplative glance before Mark opened the door. "This way, ladies," he said and they followed him inside.

Mark led them down the hallway and to the elevator. Once inside, he pressed the button for the eighteenth floor. Veronica felt pinpricks along her spine as the cab rose and Jenna concentrated on her breathing. The ding was followed by an abrupt stop as the doors slid open. Their future was merely steps away.

Mark marched purposefully down the hall and stopped at room 1801. "Jenna, Parker is waiting inside. I'll be back in an hour to bring you to the announcement broadcast." He slid the card into the slot and the door clicked. With a last glance at her friend, she pressed inside.

"This way," Mark said as Veronica forced her feet to move. A few paces later, they stopped at room number 1803. Following the same moves, he released the latch and said, "Cameron is already here. I'll see you in an hour."

"Thank you," she replied to his retreating back.

AS JENNA ENTERED THE ROOM, Parker rose from a table that was situated by the window. Upon it, a tall white taper glowed against the evening skyline and a few other candles shone brightly upon side tables. Red rose petals littered the floor and a king-sized bed. A table covered in white with two silver domes resting upon it explained the tasty aroma that nearly overshadowed Parker's tempting cologne.

Jenna's heart jumped at the sight of him in a tailored grey suit. His expression was serious, which made her wary. His voice was soft as he said, "Jenna, you look beautiful as always." He came to her, pulling her into a tight hug that made her want to cry. She'd missed him terribly. They stayed that way for a time, holding each other closely and savoring the moment.

Parker's voice vibrated through his chest. "Can we talk?"

Reluctantly, she tilted her head to face him, "Yes."

He pulled a chair out for her and handed her a glass of wine.

"Thank you," she said and took a sip.

"How have you been?" he asked.

Deliberately, she placed the glass on the table and replied, "I've been okay. What about you?"

His eyes glimmered in the candlelight and his reply turned her to liquid. "You've been missing from me."

She inhaled sharply and reveled in the fact that their feelings were mutual. Before she could respond, Parker continued.

"Listen, I have something to tell you. I hope you won't be upset with me. I made a decision that affects us both and I should have discussed it with you. I tried to, but I knew leaving the letter already crossed the line. With the rules of the test, and everything," his eyes trailed to the distant buildings, "I couldn't."

Tears threatened to betray her but she remained stoic and braced herself for what he had decided.

"I spoke to the Fosters about our situation."

Jenna's eyes grew wide. "You what?"

"I know it was risky, but when I went in to resign, they asked why. You know how nosy Nancy can be, so I told her about the Love Test."

"Oh my god. When did you do this?"

"Last week."

Jenna thought back to her workweek and realized it explained some of the dreamy looks had Nancy sent her way and the smirk that John seemed to hold during a few of their conversations. "What did they say?"

"They didn't let me resign."

"But you technically work on my team."

"I know. I reminded them of that."

"And?"

"They asked if I could handle the fact that they selected you over me for the promotion."

Jenna's eyes went downcast as she fiddled with the stem of her wine glass.

"I told them it was no problem for me."

Her eyes met his and she asked the question she wasn't sure she wanted the answer to. "Is it a problem for them?"

He chuckled then, a welcoming sound that caused Jenna's heart to palpitate. "They laughed and reminded me that they met at work too. It's a family business and they said we're a part of the family. They were supportive."

Jenna couldn't believe her ears. She could have been upset with him for putting them both on a limb without talking to her first, but she understood his reasons and was honored that their relationship meant so much to him that he was willing to resign to pursue it. "So, we're okay at work?"

Parker tilted his head to one side, "I'm sure there will be some talk, but I won't tolerate it and neither will Nancy or John. They picked you because you're the right person for the job. They said they want to create a workplace that is equitable for everyone and we're both valued team members."

Jenna rose to her feet, nearly knocking the table in her haste. Parker met her fervor and their lips met in their steamiest kiss yet.

━━

VERONICA EASED INTO THE ROOM, taking half steps as Cameron rose from sitting at the edge of the bed.

"V, you look sexy as always." Cameron wore a dark suit and a white shirt as he peered at her through narrowed eyes.

"Thank you, Cameron. I like your suit."

"Give me a hug," he demanded softly.

She obliged, feeling the strength of his muscles as he held her close. After a time, he pulled back and, holding both of her wrists, he said, "I need to clear things up with you."

Her sharp inhale caused Cameron to backpedal slightly. "First, why don't we have a toast."

Veronica didn't feel like toasting, but she did want some alcohol. Cameron handed her a glass from the table as she contemplated the view. Cars moved swiftly and buildings glistened with too many lights considering many were office suites vacated for the evening. He stood beside her and tapped his glass to hers, "To starting over, the right way."

Veronica's gaze was searing. Her eyes narrowed to slits as the words spilled out unchecked, "How many times should we start over Cameron?"

He exhaled and looked at his feet. "I'm sorry about New Year's Eve. I didn't expect her to call me."

"Why not? From the sound of it, you've kept in close contact over the years."

"Not close contact. We just stayed in touch."

Veronica walked to the window and watched a plane circle in the distance. "You didn't stay in touch with me. Not once did you reach out. I guess you had nothing to say."

"No," he shook his head and pulled at her arm, "I had too much to say. Things I didn't know how to express. I was afraid and I thought there was no hope. I know I fucked up and it was bad of me to give any of the blame to you. I made the choice to follow my career and Kyra was a minor piece of my confusion. It didn't last and I don't love her. I love you."

Veronica's heart dropped. The words she'd longed to hear had been released into the air and the chance to respond in kind was once again before her, but she couldn't say it back. "How can I believe you? You've been lying all along."

"Not lying. I just didn't tell you she and I stayed friends."

"Why not?"

He rolled his eyes. "You know why I didn't say anything, Veronica. I wasn't trying to be sneaky but I knew you'd be upset. I should have told you, even if it caused problems, but I didn't want to risk...us being in this situation."

"Is that how it will always be between us? Any time a contentious subject comes up, you'll hide it from me rather than deal with a conflict?"

He breathed deeply and looked defeated. "What can I say, V? I'm sorry. It won't happen again."

Veronica felt defeated. Her anger was no longer carrying her and instead it was replaced by a lightness that made her feel faint. Her thoughts ran to Troy and the fact that she didn't tell Cameron of his declaration. She was no different than he after hiding that development, a fact that had troubled her for weeks. Why didn't she tell him? She could blame the Love Test rules, or use his excuse of not wanting to create problems that didn't exist, but was that the reason she'd kept it to herself?

"I have an idea," Cameron stated.

She met his gaze. "Why don't we eat some dinner and try to relax before they call us down?" he continued.

Though food was unappealing, a reprieve from the topic sounded great. "Okay."

———

RYAN AND LANIE arrived at the Hotel Monaco with a few minutes to spare before the decision broadcast. As they neared the spot where the first met, Ryan stopped Lanie and said, "I owe Erve my life for making me take this assignment. It's like Serge said, a moment of chance turned our worlds upside down."

Lanie's eyes grew wide and she exclaimed, "That's it!"

Ryan quirked his head, "What's it?"

"The baby's name."

"You want to name the baby, Chance?"

"Do you like it?"

"I do, but what if it's a girl? Do you think it would work?"

"Sure, why not? But it is a boy."

Ryan placed his hand on Lanie's stomach and mouthed, "Chance Glass. That's a great name." Her belly hardened under his fingers. "Woah, that was crazy."

Lanie strived to gain her breath, "Yes, it's been happening all day. I'm sure it's Braxton Hicks."

"Does it hurt?"

She shook her head, "Not really. It feels strange, that's all."

His eyes grew wide and he wondered how he was going to handle seeing her in pain during the birth. "Are you sure?"

"Yes, now let's go before we're late. I'm excited to see what happens with the couples."

"Yes, boss," he agreed and they walked toward the event, following the steps they took once before.

"There you are," called Shelly. "I was getting worried."

"Sorry, Shelly," Ryan apologized. "We were running a little late."

"Not to worry. You're right on time and Lanie, look at you! How do you do it?"

"Thank you, Shelly. I love your suit."

"Ah, this old thing?" She laughed and continued talking as they walked toward a private room. "When is the baby due?"

"Next Tuesday," Lanie replied.

"How exciting, " she said. "Here we are," she said as she opened the door. "We have a few minutes to meet and go over things before the broadcast."

Ryan and Lanie joined Shelly at a round table and reviewed the paperwork she'd organized. "Here are the questions you planned. I love your idea of having Lanie start and you asking the final question. Remember it's being streamed live. We'll cue you so you know which direction to look and we'll also have cards near the camera so you can read the questions if you need reminding. How are you feeling?"

Lanie nodded and said, "I'm ready," ignoring the fact that her abdomen had tightened again.

Ryan agreed, "Got it."

"Okay, I'll be back soon."

⸻

A KNOCK at the door set Parker and Jenna straight. It was time to go to the verdict ceremony. Parker strode across the room and held the door for Jenna. They stepped into the hallway and watched Mark as he rapped against the door two away from their room.

⸻

CAMERON AND VERONICA stood and walked to the door. Instead of discussing their decision further, they had used the time to have dinner, acting as if their fate as a couple wasn't hanging in the balance.

⸻

"LANIE, Ryan, we're ready for you," Shelly said from the doorway.

Ryan helped Lanie to standing and kissed her cheek before they followed her prompts. "This way," Nancy said and walked purposefully toward the stage.

They entered the packed room and a raucous round of applause was underway. Looking toward the stage, they could see that the couples were already seated. The women were in the center with the men on either side.

Lanie squelched a bit of nerves and another contraction as they edged up the set of stairs to join them. Their microphones were activated as the announcer bellowed, "Welcome to the hosts of the first annual www.lovetest.love match event, destiny's pair, Ryan and Lanie Glass."

They followed Nancy's prompts and sat in the seats opposite the couples. Lanie took the inside, facing Parker and Jenna. Ryan was near the audience, facing Cameron and Veronica. Nancy waved and pointed in the direction of the spectators. Ryan and Lanie waved.

This got the crowd howling. Ryan held up a hand. "Happy Valentine's Day, everyone. We're just as excited as you are to be here tonight. I, for one, can't wait to hear how it turns out for these great people."

Lanie chimed in, "I'm not waiting any longer! Parker, I have a question for you," she said.

"Okay," his voice broke.

"If you could choose one word to summarize your www.lovetest.love experience, what would it be?

Parker took an inhale and contemplated the ceiling.

"The first word that enters your mind."

He looked from Jenna to Lanie and said, "Mate."

A chorus of high-pitched squeals came from the audience and even from Veronica. Lanie found herself smiling between the Braxton Hicks.

She faced Jenna. "Jenna, what was your favorite date and why?"

Jenna flushed at the call of her name and stared at her own feet. After a beat, with almost a defiant look on her face she answered, "Our weekend in Bend was my favorite date because that's when Parker and I really got to know one another."

"OOOHHHH" was the collective moan from the on lookers.

Lanie shifted in her seat to look toward Veronica. The position proved no more comfortable. "Veronica, if you had to do it over, would you go through this www.lovetest.love experience again?"

Veronica's voice was soft as she replied, "I would."

The audience hooted and clapped in response.

"And Cameron, do you feel this process changed you in any way?"

He looked from Lanie to Veronica. There was hope in his dark eyes. "I have changed after this. I've learned from my mistakes and I won't mess up again."

"AAAWWWEEE." The audience presented a range of sounds.

Lanie rested a hand on Ryan's knee and her fingers dug slightly. He looked at her but saw no signs of strain on her face. He assumed it was nerves.

"Now I'm going to ask a couple of questions. This first one is a question for each couple. I'll give you a few seconds to confer and respond. Don't forget to cover your mics so we can't hear you. Are you ready?"

They nodded vaguely.

"What was something difficult that came up during this process and how did you deal with it? Let's start with Parker and Jenna, please."

Parker covered his microphone and turned toward Jenna. "I think the answer is kind of obvious, but we can't tell them what we decided."

"Agreed," she replied.

Parker suggested, "Why don't you answer for us?"

"No, you tell them what the problem was and I'll tell them how we handled it."

"Okay," his eyes held for a fraction then he turned to

face Ryan. "The hardest situation we've had to deal with has been our workplace conflict."

The audience screeched.

Jenna cleared her throat and with a somber expression said, "We've dealt with it as best we could."

Ryan nodded and redirected to Cameron and Veronica. Their heads were close and their hands over the mic. Cameron said, "How do we answer?"

Veronica contemplated his mouth and reminded herself how much they'd once shared. "You say: The past has been hard for us to deal with."

He didn't look pleased as he turned to face Ryan. "What's been hard on us is what we always struggled with. The problems of the past, I guess." This he said in Veronica's direction, "But they won't be a problem anymore."

Ryan looked toward Veronica, who remained silent. The audience grew still.

"This is the final question of the night. After this, it's time to party."

The crowd cheered heartily.

He asked, "Parker and Jenna, was the www.lovetest.love match successful? Have you met your match?"

The room was hushed as Parker and Jenna stared into each other's eyes. After a few seconds, they turned to face Ryan, and Parker spoke first. "Jenna is the best woman I've ever known and I only hope she'll give me the chance to be her match. I'm in love with her."

The walls vibrated with a deafening boom of praise for his declaration.

Jenna's eyes misted and she said, "He is the best man I've ever known and I only hope he'll give me the chance to be his match. I'm in love with him."

The screams and applause were uproarious. Jenna and

Parker ignored it all and kissed as if they were the only people in the room.

Ryan tried to bring the crowd down a notch so he could ask the question of couple number two. It takes Parker and Jenna's release to calm them down. After few errant yells that can't be contained, he managed, "Cameron and Veronica, same question. Was the www.lovetest.love match a success? Did you meet your match?"

Veronica shifted in her seat to face Cameron when something, nay someone in the audience caught her eye. Just past his shoulder, Troy stood near the side exit. The whites of his eyes shot toward her, stealing her tongue.

Cameron confessed, "I've made so many mistakes, in the past and during this process, but I think we met twice for a reason. It seems we're meant to be together."

His voice brought her forward. Like an echo his words reverberated against her greatest disappointment and she knew it wouldn't be the worst, unless she made the same mistake again. Her consideration was lengthy as the audience had grown mute with anticipation. The side door opened and closed. Troy was gone.

Her throat creaked as she said, "No. No. I have to go." She stood and in a flurry of movement and gasps, ran in platform heels off the stage and down the stairs. The crowd opened an aisle for her to weave through as she made her way for the side exit door.

The spectators milled awkwardly as Cameron removed his microphone and rose from his chair. His exit wasn't nearly as dramatic as he was ushered behind stage by Shelly.

Ryan and Lanie tried to rebound. Ryan cleared his throat. "Well, this is what live broadcasts are about. As you can tell, none of us were prepared for that." He stood and pulled Lanie to her feet, facing the camera he said, "On behalf of the www.lovetest.love group, Lanie, and myself, join us in congratulating Parker and Jenna on their newfound romance. Best wishes, you two."

The crowd clapped and so did Lanie and Ryan. Another contraction took over and this one, Lanie couldn't mask. Mid-clap, she felt a trickle of water and to her embarrassment, a puddle had pooled between her legs. Ryan's eyes grew wide at the sight and his face concerned.

"Is that?"

She put on a grimace-smile, "Yes, my water broke."

"Oh my god," he exclaimed. "Let's go. We have to go."

The audience gasped.

"Ryan…"

"What? Stop talking, let's go."

"Your microphone. It's on."

He peered around the room and every face confirmed the obvious truth. "Sorry, everyone, but as you can see, we have to go. Enjoy the party."

He wiped his hands along his pants then swiftly removed their microphones before helping Lanie down the stairs and out the side door.

Parker and Jenna looked at one another, as did the crowd. Removing her microphone then his, Parker said, "Shall we?"

She took his hand and with the clearest eyes, Jenna said, "Yes."

They scurried down the stairs and out the side exit. When they arrived outside, they found Troy and Veronica helping Lanie and Ryan into the car. "Wait for us," Jenna called.

Jenna and Parker climbed into the limo as Ryan warily watched Lanie. "Are you in pain?" he asked.

No longer trying to hide the contractions, Lanie

gripped Ryan's hand and breathed shallowly. "It doesn't feel great."

He ran a hand through his hair. "I'm sorry. Today was too much."

She replied through gritted teeth, "You think you're to blame for the agony of childbirth?"

Ryan's eyes grew wide as he inhaled and decided to remain quiet.

———

VERONICA RODE in the front with Troy, from time to time stealing a glance at him as he deftly maneuvered to the hospital. He was calm and decisive as he ran vacant red lights and determined the quickest route. She marveled at his steadiness after the events of the day and at her own after what happened between her and Cameron. She'd walked away from the dream of her past and this time for good.

They approached the long, steep road that led to the emergency room and Troy finally spoke, "I'll park the car and find you."

He ran around the car to help Parker and Jenna assist Lanie's exit. Ryan found an abandoned wheelchair at the entry and pulled it over. Lanie tried to wave him off but was overtaken by a strong contraction.

"Please, Lanie, sit," Ryan begged.

With and Jenna's aid, she lowered into the seat and Ryan spirited her inside. Troy called, "I'll park and be back."

Jenna, Parker and Veronica remained. Instinctively, Jenna put her arm around Veronica and said, "Let's go inside and wait." Their arms linked and three-wide, they entered the hospital. Ryan nervously scrawled their insurance information as he managed the clipboard and Lanie squirmed in the chair.

"Are you okay?" Jenna asked Lanie.

She inhaled strongly, "Yes, but I think I've changed my mind about the drug-free delivery."

Jenna laughed nervously. "I fully intend to dope up when my time comes."

Veronica looked anxious. "Sorry we tagged along. It sort of happened."

Lanie managed a laugh, "Trust me, I know that the Love Test has a mind of its own. You may as well stay and see how it turns out. It's only fair."

Veronica smiled for the first time all day. "I guess that's true."

"Besides, Ryan likes having his best friend close by." Lanie looked over Veronica's shoulder and called, "Troy, glad you made it back so quickly."

Veronica felt her heart skip as Troy's intense eyes flashed from Lanie to her.

Lanie winced then managed, "Did you know that Troy and Ryan are good friends? They met years ago when he was on assignment."

Veronica was surprised to learn that and wondered just how much destiny was involved in her and Troy's acquaintance. She knew it wasn't the time but she would get to the bottom of it.

"Glass," called a nurse in scrubs who had just come out from behind the door.

"That's us," Ryan rushed past Lanie's wheelchair. "My wife is in labor."

The motherly expression on the blonde nurse's face said she'd seen it all and he was nothing new. "I see that, Mr. Glass. Let's bring her in for an examination. This way."

She smiled easily and marched forward as Ryan grappled with the chair. "We'll be waiting," called Jenna.

Ryan waved absently as they disappeared behind the door.

The four of them stood awkwardly. Parker was the only one unaware of the budding romance between Troy and Veronica. Jenna turned toward Parker. Their eyes met and a well of love burst from her as she finally let it sink in. He was her match and as much as she tried to avoid it, to rationalize it away, there was no denying they fit. Suddenly, the need to be alone with him overtook her. She also knew that Veronica and Troy had things to discuss.

"Troy, why don't you and V go to the cafeteria and have a chat. Parker and I would like to talk as well. Could we have the keys to the car?"

Troy tried to suppress the smirk that flashed across his mouth as he fished the keys from his pocket and handed them to Jenna. "I parked close to the entrance, section A."

Parker cleared his throat as Jenna tossed, "Thanks, see you guys later."

Veronica watched her scurry through the double doors, presumably to have sex in the limo. That left her and Troy alone.

"The café is this way," he announced and slowly walked that direction.

Veronica's high heels clicked as she walked beside him down the long hallway. They arrived at the cafeteria and Troy asked, "What do you want?"

She shook her head, "Nothing, really. Water?"

He nodded, "Find a seat. I'll be right over."

She surveyed the space. Wooden booths were situated around the perimeter with tables down the center. Fortunately, it wasn't crowded. Veronica took a seat in an empty corner.

Troy looked serious as he crossed the room carrying two water bottles. He unscrewed the lid and placed one in front of Veronica and did the same with his own, taking a sip before pinning her with his eyes. "Here we are."

She found his snarky tone frustrating. "Do you have anything to say?"

He teased, "Say?"

Her eyes narrowed to slits as she tossed, "Yes, say!" Veronica was peeved. She'd publicly walked out on Cameron after Troy wrote her a note. It was hasty and rash and based on his reaction, possibly the dumbest thing she'd ever done.

He shook his head, no.

Veronica lost her mind. Was he playing a game? She knew she couldn't remain seated next to him without making a scene. She stood abruptly, bumping the table as she did.

Troy was quick to follow. He grabbed her wrist with determined pressure. She couldn't move and instead turned to face him. Without warning his luscious lips were upon hers, brushing away her thoughts with his tender swipes. He assaulted her mouth with feather light blows until she was senseless with desire. Their first kiss foretold that what was between them would smother the pains of their pasts.

———

PARKER OPENED the door and Jenna pounced, pulling him inside the car. "Lock the door," she demanded while rapidly unbuttoning his shirt.

He pressed the button and tossed the key fob aside. His mouth sought hers and his hands tangled in her long blonde hair.

Jenna tugged Parker's jacket and shirt away, exposing his bubbling abs and chest. He looked like a guy from the cover of one of those romance books her mom used to read and she was ecstatic about it. "Sit," she commanded and pushed him against the back seat.

He pulled her toward him and wrapped his arms around her waist, keeping her on his lap. She lowered her mouth to meet his and their tongues found a galaxy of exploration. They moaned together, their desire mounting with every kiss.

He fondled her breasts, then pulled her shirt off. The gold bra she wore barely encased her jewel shaped nipples. His fingers wandered as she grappled with his belt buckle. With it finally undone, she kneeled between his legs and looked him in the eye. Her lips curved as her fingers hooked either side of his pants. She tugged and they dropped to his ankles.

Parker's expression was wary and excited. To his joy and disbelief, Jenna ducked her head and took him. With one move, she managed to resort him to shudders. Her mouth was knowing and not in the least bit timid. He was certain he was dreaming. It had to be a fantasy, the way she commanded him. He'd do anything for her and as much as he wanted to let go, he had to have her. He tugged her hair slightly and with the most indecent sloth, Jenna smoothed her tongue from his hungry member until his grip upon her wrist told her to stop. His tone was gravel, "Jenna, come here."

She leaned back from hands and knees and shimmied out of her underpants. Parker pulled her up and skimmed his hands along her thighs, lifting her skirt and finally cupping her bottom. He slouched in the seat and lifted her until his lips met her lower ones. His teases were corrupt. Almost imperceptibly he used his tongue to encourage her, but his retreat was so fast, she couldn't be sure it had really happened. His nose rested against her tiny bush and his tongue took liberties along her line. His fingers around her hips grounded her. She never thought she'd enjoy being possessed, but Parker changed that. His mouth demanded more and she was filling up. Needing to come with him, she held the orgasm at bay.

"Parker," she spoke in jagged breathes, "I want you."

He pulled her to straddle him and she happily obliged. Their eyes met, and love and lust simmered as they bonded. He felt every part of her as she held him captive.

Her head tipped back and Parker's lips affixed to her hardened nipple, biting gently as she throbbed around him. He knew he would explode at any moment. Then he felt it. The rumbling came from deep inside her. It moved from his shaft to her throat as she began to scream and he lost himself in the eruption that was their destiny.

THE MONITOR BEEPED CEASELESSLY as everyone hovered around Lanie. One nurse checked the numbers while the doctor encouraged her to push from between her legs. Ryan's hand was nearly crushed by Lanie's tight grip. Sweat poured from her as she gritted her teeth and bore down. She collapsed against the pillows and nearly wept. "I can't."

"You can," encouraged the doctor. "It's crowning. Just a few more pushes and you can rest."

Another contraction overcame her and Ryan helped her forward and whispered near her ear. "You're amazing, Lanie."

She scoffed as the contraction peaked.

"Push," commanded the doctor and the nurse flanked her other side.

"A little longer," the nurse asked. "That's right, keep pressing."

The traumatic sounds his wife made tormented Ryan. If he could do this for her, he would. He knew he would never make her do it again. Ignoring the nausea in his gut, Ryan continued to let Lanie crush his hand.

The doctor announced, "The head is out. Only one more push and your child is born."

She was exhausted to near delirium. All Lanie wanted to do was go to sleep, but the pain wouldn't let her. A shock of agony hardened her stomach and separated her center. It felt like she was severed to her clavicle. She knew she'd never be the same after this and she wanted the pain to stop.

"Now, push," demanded the doctor.

The nurse was quick to chime in, "Last push, you can do it."

Ryan observed the scene as if he were floating in the room. His wife's face was mashed unrecognizable as she squelched and bore down, eliminating their child from her center. The ground rushed up and he was gone. A scream in the background and repeated taps against his cheeks roused him from his escape.

He looked dazed as the nurse hovered over him, "You fainted."

Shaking himself to reality, Ryan was mortified as he grappled to stand. Thankfully, the nurse was there to assist. "You okay?"

He remained silent as he sat up, still feeling disoriented. "Let me help you," said the nurse.

Ryan stood and practically dove to Lanie's side. In her

arms was their swaddled child. "Are you, all right?" he asked.

Her face was transformed to serene as her eyes met his. "Chance, this is your Daddy. He's a bit squeamish. Otherwise he's a good guy."

Ryan kissed Lanie's hair and with the most-timid stroke, he touched their child's cheek with his finger. "Is it?"

"A boy," Lanie announced. "We have a son." Tears shone in her eyes and Ryan's expression was awe.

———

PARKER AND JENNA composed themselves as best they could before returning to the lobby of the emergency room. Troy and Veronica were already seated and looking quite cozy. Parker noticed that Troy was holding Veronica's hand. He looked at Jenna and she whispered, "I forgot to mention, there's something going on between V and Troy."

"Hmm. I guess she won't be mourning Cameron for long."

Jenna snickered, "Does that upset you?"

"Not at all. I never had a strong feeling about him, but I didn't see this coming."

"It was a surprise, even to Veronica."

"Hey, guys," Parker said as they approached and took the seats next to them.

"Have you heard anything yet?" Jenna asked.

Veronica's expression was dazed and happy, as if she'd just awoken from a good dream. "No, not yet."

The wait wasn't long before Ryan popped his head through the door saying, "You're still here."

They all stood and walked toward him, "Yes, how is she?"

"Come in and see for yourselves," Ryan held the door and waved them in. They waited for him to lead them down the busy corridor. There were moans, beeps, and medical professionals rushing around. They traveled down one hall and took a turn. "We're in here."

He entered and the group filed in behind him. Their hushed steps roused Lanie from her doze. The tiny bundle of new life was clutched protectively in her arms. She smiled through swollen lips and greeted, "The gang's all here."

"Wow," Jenna exclaimed. "You look amazing."

"Seriously," Veronica chimed. "How do you do it?"

Lanie sneered, "You've got to be kidding. I could care less though. Look at this little boy. Isn't he perfect?"

"A boy," Troy said and his mouth cracked in a giant smile. "Congratulations, friend," he hugged Ryan, patting him aggressively on the back.

"Congratulations, both of you," Parker said.

Veronica and Jenna hovered closely around Lanie. "Would you like to hold him?"

In a most uncharacteristic reaction, Veronica's eyes misted as she managed, "Yes, please."

Lanie's smile was radiant as she gingerly passed her precious son to Veronica. Troy came to stand behind her and his expression matched the occasion. A miracle was in their midst and the world was, for the moment, a glorious place.

"What's his name?" asked Jenna.

Ryan smiled at his wife and said, "Chance Madoc Glass."

Troy's eyes met Ryan's. "A tribute to your friend," he said.

Ryan's lips went stern as he took it all in. For a moment he felt Madoc with them.

The door flew open and Audrey bounded inside. "Let me see. Let me see," she demanded softly as she pushed everyone out of the way. Her tear-streaked face gleamed under the florescent lights as she looked from her friend to the infant and back. "You did it!"

"It seems," Lanie replied.

"Oh, look at him! I knew it was going to be a boy." Without requesting she reached for the baby and practically snatched him from Veronica's arms.

"Audrey," Lanie said, "that's Veronica," she waved her hand in gesture, "Parker, and Jenna. You already know Troy."

This was the first time Audrey stopped looking at the baby. "Yes, I do," she batted her lashes in his direction. "Nice to meet you all in person," she said to the other three. "I've heard a lot about you."

They looked at each other. "Well," Parker suggested, "maybe we should go and let you get some rest."

Jenna held his hand as Troy pressed Veronica's back and they made for the door. "Thanks for letting us meet Chance," Veronica said while looking back.

"I'm glad it worked out the way it did," Lanie called.

Ryan came to sit beside Lanie and Audrey did too. "Baby Chance," Audrey spoke and his eyes flickered, "happy birthday, little one. I'm your Auntie Audrey."

A shocking explosion of tears and a gasp expelled from Ryan as he broke down out of sheer joy. "This is the happiest moment of my life. Thank you," he said to Lanie and kissed her hard.

"As you can see," Audrey taunted, "Daddy's a bit of a drama queen and Mommy is a sucker for his kissing."

10

LOVE IS IN THE AIR

Ryan and Lanie's Second Wedding Anniversary

SUMMER ARRIVED A FEW WEEKS EARLY, as a delightfully warm breeze danced with the sun, setting an idyllic scene for Ryan and Lanie's second wedding anniversary. The enormous canopy tent was installed in the Mains' back yard as a precaution against the testy Portland weather. The lawn was alive as the group, including Audrey, Ron, Jay, Serge, Ryan's three brothers, Thomas Main, Bobby, Ryan, Troy, Parker, and Drew, Lanie's dad, all played bocce ball. In a traditional and sexist fashion, the ladies were enjoying time sitting together under the shade of a giant oak and sipping various libations.

Annette Main looked like a queen as she sat in her special chair, wearing a floral dress and matching lavender hat. She smiled at the group and demanded, "Lanie, give me that child. My arms are getting lonely over here."

Lanie stood and carried the squirmy baby to sit on her lap, "Be a good boy, Chancey."

His oversized eyes focused on Annette Main's then gravitated toward her hat. At only four months old, he was starting to reach for things. She spoke sweetly as she teased, "Tell her you don't need reminding to be a good boy. You already are one."

A smile cracked on the boy's drooling lips and his blue eyes beamed with delight. Rani Blackwell came to stand beside Annette and together they cooed at the grandchild they'd silently agreed to share. Lee and Lily pranced around happily looking at the "baby" with the condescension of toddlers. By now, Lee was nearly four and Lily, already two. To them, Chance was a baby and they no longer were.

The dogs set out in a pack, running toward the barbershop quartet group that had attended the baby shower. Jay and Serge marched across the lawn to greet them. Troy and Parker milled nervously around. They seemed to be conferring about something, which Jenna and Veronica didn't miss.

"What's going on?" Veronica called.

Jay waved and approached the ladies. "We have a little surprise. Since you didn't mind us stealing your thunder during the baby shower, we figured you wouldn't be too upset if we crashed your anniversary with a wedding of our own."

"What?" Lanie gasped and stood.

"That's right," Serge chimed. "If you are okay with it, we're getting married today, right now, in front of all of our dearest friends. We couldn't imagine a luckier day. This guy," he pointed to the leader of the band, "is going to officiate."

The ladies clapped vigorously as the men approached doing the same. "Well done," Ryan exclaimed.

"But first," Jay announced, "Troy and Parker ask that

Veronica and Jenna join them here." He waved his hand to a spot in front of the band.

The ladies lurched forward as the Barber Shop Quartet began singing the Bruno Mars song, "Marry You." Parker took Jenna's hands and as her mouth gaped, he dropped to one knee. Veronica was so focused on them that she initially didn't notice Troy kneeling in front of her. The lyrics danced around the question, whose answer they would all bear witness to. They echoed: "...baby, I think I wanna marry you."

Troy looked intense and nervous as he held Veronica's fingers. His tone was somber as he said, "You captivated me from the start. Your style, your sass, your smarts—I love everything that comes with you. Marry me?"

He held a shiny ring in his hand and a hopeful expression on his face. He was her man and she knew it. "I will marry you but only because I love you."

He crushed his lips to hers and they sealed their agreement.

Parker's translucent eyes pled and his throat was hoarse as he said, "You are the partner I always want by my side and the most beautiful woman I've ever known. Say you'll be mine, forever. Marry me?"

Jenna's eyes brimmed and her hand shook along with her head as she nodded, "Yes, Parker. I'll marry you."

He slid on the ring and as he stood, she jumped into his arms. Dress be damned, she wrapped her legs around his waist and kissed him senseless.

The party went wild and the band joined in to cheer. When the couples finally pulled apart, there were ooh's and ah's as their rings were examined and slaps of congratulations abounded. After a few minutes, Jay called the group to attention. "I need some assistance, please."

They became quiet.

"Lanie, would you do me the honor of giving me away?"

"I'd be honored!" she cried.

"Audrey, Ron, can we borrow Lee and Lily? We need a ring bearer and a flower girl."

"Of course," Audrey jumped up and down. Ron nodded.

"Great, let's get started."

He handed a basket of flowers to Lily. "When the music starts, walk toward Uncle Serge and drop these flowers along the way."

She nodded seriously.

Jay then gave Lee a pillow with the rings tied atop. "When it starts, follow your sister and stand by Uncle Serge."

The band started humming the wedding march as their leader stood in front of Serge. The toddlers started their walk, Lily haphazardly dropping golden petals along the way. Lee stared reverently at the rings and walked slowly to the front. When Lanie and Jay stopped, they hugged and Lanie whispered, "We are so fortunate and we deserve it. Best wishes, my friend."

Jay kissed Lanie's cheek and he wiped a tear from his own before facing his groom and the words that would bond them for the rest of this lifetime. Ryan's arm rested around Lanie and everyone gathered closely to watch the miracle of faith that united Serge and Jay. It took a stroke of divinity to bring this blend of people together who all learned that love conquers everything.

Also by Holly Manno